ORPHANS PREFERRED

"Wanted: Expert riders, willing to risk death daily." A boy in a hurry to be a man, Sean Callahan answers the call of the Pony Express. With a little help from his Uncle Jim—and the Navy Colt .36—Sean fights Indians and outlaws to get the mail through.

JIM MILLER

ORPHANS PREFERRED

Complete and Unabridged

LINFORD
Leicester

First published in the USA in 1985 by
Ballantine Books,
New York

First Linford Edition
published March 1988
by arrangement with
Ballantine Books,
New York

Copyright © 1985 by James L. Collins
All rights reserved

British Library CIP Data

Miller, Jim
 Orphans preferred.—Large print ed.—
 Linford western library
 Rn: James L. Collins   I. Title
 813'.54[F]   PS3563.I412/

 ISBN 0-7089-6493-1

LT W   12 95
Miller, Jim.
Orphans preferred

Published by
F. A. Thorpe (Publishing) Ltd.
Anstey, Leicestershire

Set by Rowland Phototypesetting Ltd.
Bury St. Edmunds, Suffolk
Printed and bound in Great Britain by
T. J. Press (Padstow) Ltd., Padstow, Cornwall

This one's for Cheryl Woodruff, who was so instrumental in editing my first three books and the first two Colt Revolver Novels. . . . Here's hoping our trails cross again.

1

FINN couldn't make it that year, so I went. It was a family tradition that was as old as I was, you might say, though that ain't saying much. Being all of fourteen, I still had me an escort, and that took all the fun out of everything. Well, almost.

Saint Louis was pretty in the early spring, and right showy too, for it had more buildings put together in one place than any other town I'd ever seen in my life. It was business I was on, but I found my mind wandering about the city and wondering what it must have been like back in '46 when my pa was killed on these streets. I never did know him, only of him, for he had been killed only a short time before I was born. But to hear the family talk, he was the kind of man you don't meet but once in a lifetime.

"You got a fella named Gadney works here?" I asked the lone man in the funeral parlor. I'd heard about these fellas and the work they did but doubted I could ever get far enough along to where I'd make a life out of dying. Besides, these fellas all tended to be tall and skinny as a string bean.

"Yes, I'm Mr. Gadney." He extended a hand that was as skinny as the rest of him. Maybe it was just me, but I couldn't remember ever feeling a piece of flesh that was clammier than his. He also gave off that smile his sort do that's meant to convey how sorry they are that you had to drop in. Maybe that would pass for those who had really lost someone, but I was here on a different matter. And the truth is, I could see in his eyes that he'd be glad to take my money, grief or not.

"What can I do for you?" he asked.

"Funny, you don't look like the fella they told me was here." I could feel my face screw up as I looked over the rest of him, for he was far younger than the man who had been described to me as running the establishment.

"You must mean my father." He paused a moment as though to collect his thoughts before he said, "He passed away last summer." There might even have been some honest grief in his words as he spoke them.

"My name's Sean Callahan." I said it like he ought to know me and got a look in return that said he was thumbing through the names he was supposed to know but couldn't find mine. "I've got a bone to pick with you."

"My, my, but aren't we uppity for such a young boy," was all he said in what I'd call an uppity voice of his own.

He was older than me, maybe in his twenties. I'd never had any real run-ins with these older types, but I knew I didn't like him. Especially his reference to me as a young boy. The only thing I knew just then was that I had been sent to check on Pa's grave, and there were a lot of people depending on me.

So I did what I thought was right.

"You know, mister," I said, slowly pulling out the Colt Navy I carried on my left hip, "Sam Colt give this to me personally a year or so back. Yup, that he did." I tried to look like I was keeping an eye on him as I checked the loads and spun the cylinder to let him see some of the shine that was still left. Maybe he could handle a dead man's body, but from what I could see in his eyes, he was having a whole lot of trouble dealing with a live human. But then a lot of people get that way when they see a gun.

"You're not going to—"

"Mister, I was just telling you that I got this as a personal gift from Sam Colt." I spun the cylinder again and gave him an innocent smile before a frown crossed my face and I let him see how mad I was getting. "Of course, I've never taken to being talked at the way you just run your mouth either." That broke him out in a cold sweat. "Now maybe *you* feel like being *uppity*, mister, but *I* feel like taking a walk 'cause I got something to show you. What do you say?"

"Well, I suppose," he said, real sheepish like. Then he glanced back toward the rear of the building at whatever it was he was doing before I'd come in. "But what about—"

"I wouldn't worry about it." I shrugged, holstering my pistol. "I hear grave robbers don't strike till after dark, so whoever is back there ought to be safe."

The graveyard wasn't but a few blocks from the funeral parlor, and I led him there, with him acting nervous all the way. When we got there, I went to the headstone that was Pa's. I knew what it was supposed to read by heart, for I'd heard the story of how he had gotten killed more times than I cared to count. "Liam Callahan, 19 July 1790–18 June 1846," it was supposed to read. "Born Irish. Lived, fought, and died American." But now only half of the headstone stood; the other half was broken away as if someone had taken a hammer to it.

"I don't know if you've got vandals around here of late or what, Mr. Gadney, but I want that stone replaced." I was doing my best to sound reasonable and businesslike at the same time.

"It'll cost twenty dollars," he said in that uppity way he had, and I'll tell you, hoss, that tore it!

I grabbed him by the shirt with both fists, even if he was a good six inches taller than me. I wasn't much more than five seven right then, and downright skinny my own self, but there's some things in life you make up for with mad . . . and I was mad.

"Mister, my brother gave your pa a gold piece worth more than a hundred dollars to take care of this headstone, and I aim to see that it gets—"

I was concentrating on his eyes so much that I forgot all about what the rest of him was doing. He pushed me away with one hand, grabbed my Navy pistol with the other, and all of a sudden I was laying flat on my back looking down the business end of my own gun. And I don't mind telling you I was scared. Not because this fella had the upper hand on me, you understand. It was because the way he had the shakes a-pointing it at me, I figured he was likely to shoot me by accident more than on purpose!

"Now the tables are turned, you wretched little bastard," he said with as much contempt as he could muster. But of a sudden his bravado was gone, and then so was he as he turned and ran, gun in hand.

Watching him go, I was still angry, but more at myself than at him now. I'd been tricked and put back in the class of being a boy again, knowing that I'd never be able to live it down if my brothers got wind of what had happened. But that feeling didn't last long when I realized what the man had said to me in parting. Then I was getting up and brushing myself off, and it didn't matter that he had my gun or that he'd knocked me down. No, it didn't matter at all. I felt the blood creeping up my neck and into my face as I ran after Gadney.

Ma said I got my middle name, Donovan, from some giant of a man who went by the moniker Doniphan. To hear my two brothers talk, he could cuss worse than both of them put together and fight just as hard. I had just a shade of red to my hair, and Ma said that it, too, was Doniphan's. Now, friend, I reckon Ma was joshing me when she said that, but if this Doniphan was willing to take on his maker or anyone else in the world, well, I knew exactly how he must have felt, for that same urge was flowing through me just then.

I caught up with Gadney just as he entered his funeral parlor. He must have heard me coming, for he turned on me with the Colt. But the man knew nothing about firearms, for the weapon wasn't even cocked. That made me feel a whole lot easier, and I knocked it from his hand. But I'd made him mad enough to fight; he hit me square in the jaw and sent me back onto the boardwalk.

I rolled to the left as he came at me and was on my feet as quick as a cat. It was one of the things my brother had taught me about being skinny. You've got to make up for it with fast, and that I was. We were both on the boardwalk now as Gadney started to circle to my left, which was his mistake. He was right in front of the big plate-glass window that advertised his fancy parlor when I hit him in the middle below the breastbone. It knocked the wind out of him and put him off balance for a couple of seconds, but that was all I needed.

I grabbed hold of both his ears and brought them all the way down to my knee until I was sure I'd made contact with his face. There was blood on my pants leg when I lowered my knee, and I pushed him back, hearing a groan of pain as tears came to his eyes. Then I hit him with a left roundhouse punch that struck right on his jaw line but only staggered him. It was the second punch from my right that sent him reeling back into the plate-glass window and through it.

I had been so determined to do him in that I wasn't aware anyone was watching us until he went through that window. That was when a woman screamed and I noticed all sorts of people taking me in. I reckon the smart thing would have been to run and just get the hell out of there, but I wasn't about to leave without having my say.

"Gadney," I said, picking up my Colt as the man sat up and placed a hand over his nose as if that would stop the bleeding, "there's something you've got to know." I don't recall how I said it, for right then all I wanted him to know was that I was mad as hell. I stepped across the broken glass and squatted down next to him. With my pistol in one hand, I grabbed a handful of his hair with the other and pulled it back until I was looking at him straight in the eye. "Don't you ever call me a bastard again, mister. *Never*. I *know* who my pa is, and he's buried right out there in that graveyard. Now, I want that stone fixed and done up proper, you understand?"

The fear in his eyes seemed to subside a bit as he looked past me in silence. When I looked over my shoulder, there was the sheriff or whoever it was that stood for the law in this town. He was a big, thick-chested man who had a look about him that reminded me of an old grizzly I'd once accidentally brought out of hibernation a couple of months too early. And since this fella wasn't looking any too pleased about the whole incident, I figured I was in enough trouble as it was. I let go of Gadney's scalp.

"Want to tell me what's going on, son?" the lawman asked, taking in the broken glass scattered about the floor, and added, "besides destruction of personal property and all." He made it clear he was addressing me, but it was Gadney who got in the first words.

"He attacked me, Sheriff!" the man said anxiously. "I want him arrested and put in jail! Now, do you hear me? *Now!*" Now that the local protection was around to take care of him, the undertaker had just as big a mouth as when I'd first met him.

"That right, son?"

"No, sir," I said. "He stole my gun, and I came after him to get it back." Then, giving Gadney a hard look, I said, "I never did take to name-calling either, for that matter."

"He's lying!" Gadney yelled, loud enough for everyone to hear. And I'll tell you, hoss, if he was baiting me, he was about to get his wish, 'cause my grip on that Navy got real tight all of a sudden.

"I think you'd better give me that gun, son." The sheriff seemed like he didn't want trouble any more than I did, but I wasn't about to turn over my gun to anyone.

"No." If I said it with determination, it was because I meant it.

"Don't go making it hard on me now, boy," the lawman said as he began to shift his hand toward his own belt gun.

"Tell you what, Sheriff," a voice said from the side, and I saw James step into view. Like always, he had his hat pushed back on his head and an easygoing air about him. Still and all, he looked kind of dangerous standing there with that big Dragoon setting on his hip and a hand resting right close to it. "I won't make it hard on *you* if you don't make it hard on *him*. That way won't none of us get hurt."

He was the spitting image of my oldest brother, Nathan Hale Callahan, Jim was, tall and big-boned with a hint of mischief about him. Only Jim, he seemed to take life a lot less seriously than his pa did. Seeing him stand there with that cockeyed smile of his must have got the sheriff to wondering if the man before him really meant it or was simply joshing him. Me, I knew better.

"You know the boy?" The sheriff nodded my way, at the same time keeping an eye on Jim, who only shrugged nonchalantly.

"He's kin. That's good enough for me." The smile on his face said that he knew just what the sheriff was thinking. Looking past the lawman, he addressed Gadney, only the smile was gone from his face now. "You know, friend, I've been to places west of here where they shoot you for calling a man a liar."

"But he's only a boy," Gadney replied in the same reckless tone, still wiping blood from his face.

"Well, now, that's where I think you overlooked something, hoss," Jim said, slowly shaking his head. "I really think you did. You see, out where Sean and me grew up, well, you might say you sort of pass childhood real quick like. Instead, you learn values. Things like saying what you mean and meaning what you say." There was a short pause as Jim's brow began to resemble one of those deep-dug fields I'd seen a Missouri mule plow up. I reckon it was the Nathan coming out in him. "And I'll tell you, mister, if you'd done to me what I heard Sean say you done to him, you'd be bleeding from a whole lot more places than your nose. And that, Sheriff," he said, his voice rising enough so the whole crowd that had gathered would hear, "that means that if Sean here says the man stole his gun, that's what happened." No doubt about it, Jim was making it clear that if someone was looking for a fight, he was willing to oblige.

The silence that followed was that deadly

kind you run across every once in a while that's just waiting for something to happen, and when it does it's usually bad. The crowd was watching for the sheriff to do something, and I don't think the sheriff was wanting to do much of anything. All I was ready to do was get the hell out of there!

"What about the grave, Sean?" Jim finally said. "Did you see it?"

"Yeah, I saw it." I gave Gadney another hard stare. "It's busted up all to hell, and this fella wants twenty dollars to fix it up."

"Not hardly," Jim said in a mixture of disbelief and denial. And who could blame him, for even the sheriff winced at the price of twenty dollars. "Those stones can't be worth more'n five, ten dollars at the most, chiseling and all."

"How 'bout that, Gadney?" All of a sudden the sheriff was taking a new interest in the undertaker's way of doing business. "Is what he says true?"

"Well . . ." He drew it out long and slow, probably figuring that being caught in a lie once that day was enough.

"Friend, you listen to me and hear me real good." Jim shot a thick finger out at the man. "You fix that headstone up proper the way it's supposed to be or next year there'll be hell to pay 'cause I'm gonna send my pa here to take a look-see at my granddaddy's grave. And mister, he's thirty years older and ten times harder than I'll ever be on the likes of you."

"He's threatening me! Do you hear that, Sheriff? He's threatening me!"

"He's right, mister," the sheriff said. "I don't like what I'm hearing. Maybe you two had just better get on your horses and—"

But Jim would have none of it.

"Sheriff, I never made an undeserved threat to a man in my life." Then, turning his attention to Gadney, he added, "Mister, you just got served a dose of fair warning. And if you got records that go back to '46, friend, I want you to show 'em to the sheriff." To the lawman he said, "My uncle, Finn Callahan, gave Gadney a gold coin worth over a hundred dollars. Sheriff. That money ought to cover my grandpa's headstone and any damages done here. If it don't, I'll be surprised."

"I'll do that, Mr. . . . Callahan?"

"James Callahan."

"In the meantime—"

"Yeah, we were about to leave town anyway. You ready to ride, Sean?"

"Sure thing."

"Then let's leave these kind folks to their civilization." He flashed a quick smile to a few of the younger ladies in the crowd as he mounted his horse. Then, with a scowl on his face, he gave a cold, hard glance to Gadney and the sheriff before saying, "I don't think I can stand it much longer."

I was ready to put my heels to the mount and get the hell out of there as fast as I could, but Jim put a quiet hand on my sleeve. I followed his lead as we took our own slow time to leave the city limits.

I don't think anyone ever did run him out of a town. But that's Jim.

2

TIME comes when a man's got to strike out on his own and do for himself. Trouble is that most of us ain't quite full-growed men when we make that decision. I had met Kit Carson out there in the Rockies while I was growing up, and he said he took off when he was younger than me, and I was all of fourteen now. There had been a whole lot of others who left home young too, but the ones I kept in my mind were my brothers, Nathan and Finn. Nathan disappeared for quite a while after he had been beaten up by the town bully and run out of town when he wasn't much older than me. He was gone nearly ten years from what I was told, and when he came back to Hartford, he took care of that bully proper like. But when he left again, it was Finn who followed him down to Texas; that was in '36, and Finn was no more than fourteen when he fought at San Jacinto with Nate.

I thought I was doing the same thing when I volunteered to check on Pa's headstone this spring, but somehow I didn't feel all that excited about it as we made camp that night. And I reckon it showed.

"Kind of hard living up to someone else's expectations, ain't it?" Jim said as he tossed some bacon into a fry pan.

"Yeah," I replied, than glanced back at him in surprise. "How did you know?"

Jim shrugged, that half permanent smile on his face.

"Reckon I felt the same way when I was your age." He tossed more bacon into the pan before saying, "Seems like a hell of a long way between hay and grass, and you just can't wait for it to be over so you can get on with life."

"Yeah," I said in agreement. "Yeah, that's right."

"And right now I'd bet even money that you're wondering how the hell you're gonna live up to your brothers' reputations after what happened today." He said it as a statement of fact and then cocked an eyebrow in my direction as though waiting confirmation of what he'd just said.

I only nodded, suddenly not in the mood to say much. The mention of what had taken place that day only brought to mind the failure I felt.

Nathan or Finn wouldn't have let such a thing happen to them; nor would Jim. Maybe I was still a boy and just trying to act like a man. Finally, I said as much to Jim.

"Acting like a man is part of being a man, Sean, if you think on it a bit. Oh, this is a land for survivors all right. But don't think you're going to spend every minute of every day fighting those knight-in-shining-armor battles like Finn tells from them books of his. Taking on responsibility and doing a hard day's work, that's manhood."

Hearing what he said took some of the edge off the way I was feeling, for it made sense.

"And trying to live up to what your brothers are?" He asked it as if it were half statement, half question.

"Yeah?"

He pulled two thick slices of bacon out of the pan, dropped them onto a plate, and, handing it to me, looked me straight in the eye. "Don't."

"Huh?"

He didn't say another word but dished up his own fixings before setting them to the side.

"Oh, almost forgot." At first I thought he would explain himself, but instead he got up and undid his bedroll, removing from it a scanty piece of cloth that he brought to the fire. Opening the cloth, he revealed a half dozen homemade biscuits that still had the smell of fresh-baked to them. "Got 'em from a widow lady while you was having that fandango with Gadney," he said, offering me half of his find. "Had a right pretty daughter, too," he added. "Yessiree."

I had no interest in any woman besides Ma just then, and more of a desire to know what it was Jim was getting at about my brothers. I said as much again.

"Eat," was his only reply between mouthfuls of food.

So we ate in silence. Those biscuits tasted so good that it seemed a shame to sop them up with bacon grease, but I did, for I'd learned to make the most of what food I had. I reckon that went right along with what Jim had said to the sheriff and Gadney earlier about passing up childhood on the frontier. You got to learning a lot of valuable lessons right off, not the least of which was that you didn't waste what you didn't have to.

Still, I couldn't get what Jim had said off my mind. It was the way of him, I reckon. He'd say something to you and let you ponder it a mite and then throw a whole new line of thought at you once you believed you had him figured out. It was unsettling, to say the least, but it did make me think.

Nathan and Finn had been on the frontier for close to a quarter of a century now, both of them having the reputation of being hard and fair men. With Finn it was a matter of being a good businessman running that freighting operation of his. He had started it with a friend when the gold fields opened up in California in '49 and was still making a successful go of it the last I had heard.

Nathan, on the other hand, well, I had grown up with him and his wife, Ellie, and their son, James. Nathan had fought Mexicans, Comanches, outlaws, and the very land itself when he had to and had won out every time. If Gadney or that sheriff back there thought Jim was joshing them about what his pa would do if he found that headstone in disrepair, they were sadly mistaken. Nathan would likely beat the man to a pulp and then skin him alive and tan his hide just for the hell of it . . . and get away with it! He was that tough.

I never had taken to studying Jim before, but I did that night over supper. He was a whole different person from his pa, yet he was the spitting image of Nathan, if you had seen the two standing side by side, as I had. Both stood well over six feet in height, were big-boned, thick-chested men with blue eyes and brown hair that had faded to a sandy color because of the amount of time they spent in the sun. The only way you could tell them apart was that there weren't as many war lines in Jim's forehead as in his pa's. And the mustache. Jim was the only Callahan I'd ever seen with a mustache. I'd often wondered about that but decided it was a fashion of the times, for there were a number of other men who had taken to growing full beards and mustaches of late.

"I knew a fella a few months back," Jim said, laying his plate to one side after he'd finished his meal. "Had him a real inn-fatuation with old John Brown, he did. Yup, figured him for a real hero." He paused a moment, but I said nothing, for Jim had gotten as good at storytelling as my brother Finn. "When he heard what happened to Brown at Harper's Ferry, well, he said he was going to do just like old John, only do it right, you see. 'Course, he was a thousand miles away from where Brown was, being out in Kansas, which is a whole different territory than that east coast. But he was determined to imitate John Brown's raid, so he did."

As quickly as he had started, Jim stopped. Like I said, it's the kind of thing he would do. For instead of finishing the story, here he was a-cleaning off his plate like there was nothing else to say!

"Well, what happened?" Sometimes I wondered if he got some kind of fun stringing people along like he did.

"I'll tell you what happened," he said, a serious look about him. "The fella got *dead*."

"But how did he—"

"He got that way 'cause he *thought* he could be another John Brown, but he *wasn't*." Usually, when he told his stories, Jim had some kind of humorous ending to them, but now he was as serious as I'd ever seen him, and I didn't know why.

"I don't understand."

"Sean, the man wasn't at Harper's Ferry. He was in Bleeding Kansas, and he was fighting a whole different breed of men." He paused a moment and then raised a finger and pointed it at me as though to make a point. "He forgot that, and it cost him his life."

I nodded, thinking I knew what he was

talking about. The stories about the bloodshed on the Kansas frontier had been a part of those gory tales passed on to us by folks riding through for a good five or six years now. Slavery had become a big issue, and men like Brown had decided to do more than simply discuss it. But what Brown had done in the last two years back east was nothing compared to the raiding that had gone on in Kansas. While Brown's followers were strict abolitionists with a cause, many of the raids in Kansas had been for the sake of plundering and looting innocent towns and people. Jim was right when he said that the man had forgotten who he was dealing with.

"What I'm getting at is that fella was trying to be something he wasn't. Do you understand?"

I nodded uncertainly. "I think so."

"That's why I said not to try measuring up to your brothers." Jim was silent for a moment, almost pensive, as he reached back in his memory and found something that was worth smiling about. "Do you know what Finn told me when I did my packing about ten years ago?"

"No."

"'You can follow that trail Becknell blazed

down to Santa Fe,' he said. 'Or ride through South Pass like Jed Smith did in '24.'" Jim had been staring off at some distant star as he spoke, but his gaze fell on me as he continued. "'But you'll never have the feeling Becknell and Smith had when they went through there the first time. They're the only ones got the right to that special feeling.' And he was right, Sean, for you can follow their trails all you want, but you'll never be who they were."

"Why did Finn tell you that?"

"Same reason I'm telling it to you now. He was your age when he lit out after Nathan, following him down to Texas. He idolized him something fierce, Sean, but it was that old storyteller your brothers talk about—Cooper Hansen, wasn't that his name?—it was him that set Finn straight on it all. Told him it was what was *inside* a man that made him do for himself, not a pistol or a rifle or a knife. I reckon that's what made you light into that Gadney fella today.

"Now, I'll tell you, Sean, you can try to be like Nathan and Finn all you want, but I'll guarantee you'll never be happy. You'll find yourself competing with them 'stead of feeling like they were your brothers. It'll sour you, and that ain't no good at all."

"But they taught me everything I know! Why shouldn't I try to be like them?"

Jim shook his head. "They didn't teach you *everything*, Sean, just the basics everyone ought to know. You see, son, it's when you pack your war bag and leave that it all becomes your own responsibility, and that's when you start finding out things for yourself. Don't try to be like your brothers, Sean. What you do instead, you see, is you go out there and find yourself a piece of trail that ain't been rid over yet and then you ride it. That way you can come back and tell 'em just how it all was, just like Becknell and Jed Smith done." Here he wagged his thick finger at me again. "And *that* will make you your own man."

There wasn't much to talk about after that, for Jim had given me enough to think about. Likely he was right, but there was still one thing bothering me, and I asked him as we were laying out our bedrolls.

"Will you tell me something, Jim?"

"Sure, if I can." He rolled out his blanket on the far side of the fire and pulled off his boots.

"Did Nathan send you along to keep an eye

on me or were you really heading this way like you said?"

"Nathan didn't send me," he said without hesitation. "Nor Ma, although I never seen her worry 'bout someone like she does you. You'd think you was her son instead of me." He smiled again briefly. "No, I just got tired of trying my hand as a miner back there in Colorado. There ain't nothing there but the same kind of crowding they got in the rush of '49. Oh, they *wanted* me to keep an eye out for you, but I didn't figure that'd be a problem."

He lay down, pulled loose the Dragoon as he drew the blanket over himself, and set his beaver hat over most of his face.

"I wonder what would have happened if you hadn't showed up today like you did?" I said it as though I were half talking to myself.

"You'd have done fine by your own self, Sean. You're a bright lad, and you've got horse sense, and for my money that's worth more'n book learning any day. Just don't tell Grandma I said that." I could hear him laugh to himself as he spoke.

"Are you sure?"

He propped himself up on an elbow, pushing back his hat.

"One thing you want to remember, Sean. What I did back there wasn't to make you look small. I did it 'cause it's what kin are for."

I didn't ask Jim any more questions after that night. I reckon I was too busy thinking on what he had told me, which seemed a powerful lot for one night.

We spent our days riding at an easy pace, killing game now and again for the fire at night, and even meeting a few strangers on the road as we went. It wasn't until the fourth day out that we veered just a tad off the trail and headed north by west instead of straight west. I had noticed that most passersby had a real urge to know what was going on, for newspapers were scarce in that territory.

"You might want to be on the lookout," one man said who had stopped at our camp. "Word has it that there's a couple of brothers name of Cahan or Keller or something that are supposed to be dangerous men. At least that's what the sheriff back in Saint Louis is a-saying."

"That so," Jim said just as calm as you please. "Well, me and my pard'll keep that in mind. Much obliged."

When the man had left and we were riding

again, Jim gave me one of his mischievous looks. "Now, there, you see, you went and got *both* of us a reputation! Why, I'll bet they figure we eat rattlesnake for breakfast and griz for supper to boot!" I knew he was only funning me, but it was only a short time later that he decided we should leave the trail and travel as outriders for a while. And I couldn't say as I blamed him.

There was no more trouble, and, taking our time, within the week we were at Saint Joseph's city limits. I'd been giving a lot of thought to what Jim had said and decided to take his advice and strike out on my own. The only problem I was having was figuring out what it was I was going to do. Mostly I was too young to do much other than be an apprentice at some blacksmith shop or livery, but I was determined to make a go of finding a job.

"You mind if we stop there for a minute?" I asked, pointing out a livery stable on the edge of town.

"Sure. These horses deserve a good feed and rubdown anyway."

When we walked the horses in, Jim gave instructions for what he wanted done with them. Meanwhile, I looked over the interior of the livery, trying to figure out how hard a job it would be if the owner needed help. When he finished with Jim, I asked him flat out if he was in need of an assistant.

"No," he said, "can't use you. 'Fraid you're too skinny for the work I've got. But take a gander at that poster over there. They've got 'em up all over town."

The poster was tacked on the door to the livery. At the top was a drawing of a horse and rider. In bold black letters beneath it were the words "PONY EXPRESS, St. Joseph, Missouri, to California in 10 days or less." Beneath that was:

WANTED

YOUNG, SKINNY, WIRY FELLOWS

not over eighteen.
Must be expert riders,
Willing to risk death daily.

Orphans preferred
Wages $25 per week
APPLY, PONY EXPRESS STABLES
St. JOSEPH, MISSOURI

Jim must have seen the look on my face, for pretty soon he was right beside me studying the poster too. I don't know what he was thinking, but I had a hundred different thoughts racing through my mind about then as I read the poster a second time. And oddly enough, a lot of them had to do with what Jim had been saying a few days back.

"You fit the description," he said, likely knowing what I was thinking. "Of course, I doubt they'd ever take me," he added with a look that was half mischievous, half serious. "After all, being twenty-three makes me an old man. Besides, I ain't nowhere close to being young, skinny, or wiry. Nope, but that description fits you, all right."

If I was grinning like a fool, it wouldn't have surprised me at all. And it wasn't from what Jim had said. Nor did I care what he had said. All I knew was that I'd found a job I might just be qualified for.

"What do you think?" he asked.

My smile broadened some more as I nodded my head to Jim.

"I think I found me a trail to set out on."

3

THERE'S times you wonder if things are put on just for you, if you know what I mean. Like the time a year or so back when I went to Santa Fe with Nathan and his wife Ellie and Ma. There always seemed to be a party of sorts going on someplace or other down there.

I never will know if it was Ma having a little fun or Nathan trying to see if he could scare the hell out of his youngest brother that caused it all. It started out innocent enough, I reckon. We were standing there watching these youngsters at what must have been a birthday party. Then all of a sudden three of the girls, pigtails and all, took a look around them, sighted me, and commenced to head straight for me! Well, hoss, I didn't know what to do, which is when I found out the first lesson of combat—whenever you get cornered, *do something*, anything . . . but don't stand still! Just then I stood still, and that was my mistake, for one of those girls, the one whose blouse must have grown as fast as she had, why, she planted a kiss right on my lips. And I'll tell you, hoss, I don't think anything has ever scared me more.

I got to turning red in all the wrong places and hadn't even been out in the sun that long, so I couldn't blame it on nature. I'd heard Nathan and Ellie and Finn tell stories of the tight spots they'd been in and got to wishing I was in one of those lead-throwing contests right then and there, for I purely didn't know what to do after that girl kissed me. Like a fool I just stood there and listened to the rest of the family laugh at the joke that had been pulled on me, whether it was accidental or on purpose.

But I'll tell you what, hoss, I got a real keen disinterest in girls right that minute. Fact is, I still felt that same way, except about Ma, of course. Now, Jim, he took real interest in the ladies and the sight of an ankle, bare or stockinged. But I'm getting ahead of myself, for the only stockinged feet I was gandering at that afternoon was the ponies outside the Pony Express stables as I headed for what looked to be their main office.

I was paying so much attention to the horseflesh, in fact, that I didn't see the other youngsters who had apparently lined up outside the doors to the office. Lordy, there must have been a hundred of them, and all talking low, a-whispering to one another like they'd just snuck away from their homes and wanted to see what it was that this so-called Pony Express had to offer. I knew that was what they were wondering, because I had the same line of thought myself.

"This where you sign up?" I asked a lad at the end of the line who wasn't much taller than me. It would be hard to describe any of the mob of young boys standing there, for it seemed as if all of them had one thing in common, and that was being gangly about the limbs and skinny everywhere else. One thing I did notice about the boy I was talking to, and that was that he didn't seem none too happy about any of this, not at all.

"Reckon," was all he said as he casually glanced over my shoulder.

We waited there maybe another hour, and each time I tried to make conversation with the lad, he closed up as tight as some of those clams Finn said he'd had to eat out on the California coast. It wasn't until they handed out forms for us to fill out that I actually got a chance to say much more to him. To tell the truth, hoss, I was feeling sorry for the boy when they handed him a pencil to fill out that form and he just stared at it, as blank as the paper in front of him.

"You need a hand with that?"

He shrugged and said, "Can't write."

Not that it was anything to be ashamed of, for there was many a man on the frontier who used nothing more than his thumb print or his presence to identify himself—at least if what Nathan said was right. Me, I'd been brought up proper even though they didn't have much in the way of schools out there at the base of the Rockies where a new town called Denver was opening up. Ma had taught Nathan and Finn to read and write, so she done the same with me, just as Ellie had done with James.

"Here, I'll give you a hand." I took the paper and pencil from him. "Now, what's your name?"

"Bernard," he said, still on the shy side. "George Washington Bernard. But you can call me Wash." When I silently wrote the information down, he asked, "Why ain't you laughing? Most folks laugh when I tell 'em my name."

"No need to," I said. "I got a brother named

Nathan Hale, and I can't say I ever found reason to laugh at being named after a famous man." I put the pencil down and stuck out my hand. "My name's Sean Callahan."

We shook hands, and I finished filling out the forms, both his and mine. When we got through, we were led out back to what looked like a supply shed of sorts. From what I could hear coming from the rear of the building, it seemed as if whoever ran this outfit was talking to the boys in groups, getting them initiated as to just what they would be doing. Wash and I took a seat along with a couple dozen others and listened to the man up front talk about what it was we were going to be paid twenty-five dollars a week to do.

"If you decide to join up after I get through with my talk, boys, you'll be working for Russell, Majors, and Waddell." He was a big man who wore a black Quaker hat and the broadcloth coat and pants that were associated with those of that faith. "I can guarantee that you'll earn every penny of your wages, for it's the mail you'll be carrying on some particular route from here to Sacramento. You'll be riding seven days a week if need be, and when you're not doing that you'll be expected to help out where it's needed.

"Now, there's one thing you might want to consider before I pass out the last form you'll have to fill out, and that is what was in that flier I assume most of you have read. Well, what it said was all fact. I've only got your word that you're as expert a rider as you claim—so far. But if any of you signed on with a bluff in mind, I'd advise you to leave right now, for I'll know it before we make our first run.

"Then there's the danger element. You'll be riding against nature as well as highwaymen and Indians who, for one reason or another, may want to put an end to your young life. Now, that may sound adventurous right now, but keep in mind that if and when that danger comes up, you'll only have one person to count on—*yourself*."

By now a handful of boys had left, knowing that the boss man would find them out eventually. But Wash Bernard was still sitting there, just as glum as when I'd first met him.

After a moment of silence the man in the Quaker hat glanced over the thinned-out audience and gave a generous smile as he reached for the forms he had mentioned. He said, "In that case, boys, welcome to the Pony Express."

At first glance the form didn't look like it was much to be concerned about, but reading it over I could see it said an awful lot about what was expected of those who rode for the Pony Express. The speaker said that what we were signing was an oath made out by Alexander Majors, one of the partners, and it struck me that I had heard his name before. If memory served me right, it was my brother Finn who had had some dealings with him in the past.

> I do hereby swear, before the Great and Living God, that during my engagement, and while I am an employee of Russell, Majors, and Waddell, I will, under no circumstances, use profane language; that I will drink no intoxicating liquors; that I will not quarrel or fight with any other employee of the firm; and that in every respect I will conduct myself honestly, be faithful to my duties, and so direct all my acts as to win the confidence of my employers. So help me God.

That was what it read, and like I said, I had little doubt that the man who wrote this was the same one Finn had known. My brother's partner had thought it humorous about Majors's hatred of profanity, him believing that a good string of cuss words made the horses or mules move faster. Still, it seemed like a fair set of rules, so I wrote my name to the document and guided Wash's hand as I showed him how to sign his name.

I was right about the building being a supply shed, for we were led in and given an issue of everything we would have to have as a rider of the Pony Express. Each of us got a red shirt and blue pants that were gaudy—not to mention oversized—to say the least. But I took them anyway because the shirt and pants I had were pretty well worn. Then there was the bugle that, according to the fella handing out the issue, would be used by each rider as a signal to the next station that he was coming, so they could have his mount ready for him when he rode in. The Bible we were given was leather bound, and someone mentioned that Majors had had them made special for his riders. So far I wasn't too keen on any of it.

It was when we got to the last item that I took a new interest in this outfit. They wanted us to ride as fast as we could to get the mail from Saint Joe to Sacramento in ten days flat, so they were pretty skimpy on what we would be carrying besides the mail and ourselves. The supply man handed us an issue of a rifle and a pistol each to carry with us. The rifle was a lightweight one, but I hardly paid any attention to it since I held a brand spanking new Colt Navy in my other hand.

By God, that shined!

"Well, now, lookee here," Jim said as I rode into camp. We had arranged to meet in the afternoon at a campsite on the outskirts of town. He had coffee on the fire as well as some pan meat cooking. And even from where I stood as I dismounted, whatever it was wrapped up and sitting next to him smelled good enough for me to know that while I was getting initiated in the Pony Express, he had been out courting the ladies again. He could be a real charmer, Jim could.

I told him all about what had happened that afternoon, from meeting Wash to getting an issue of an extra Colt pistol.

"They want us to carry only one," I said as Jim put some meat on my plate and handed it to me, "but as light as I am, I figure I can carry this second one and it won't hold me back none for getting the mail through on time."

"Good thinking," Jim said through a mouthful of food. "There's some rough country you're going to be traveling through out there, and the more firepower you've got, the better off you'll be."

We ate in silence then, and I found myself staring at the shiny pistol that lay before me. I'd set it atop the clothes, bugle, and Bible, taking in its every feature. Not that I had to, you understand, for I knew that pistol by heart, knew every bit of it.

My own Navy was a Second Model 1851, a few personal copies of which Sam Colt must have set aside, for I'd not received mine until last year, nearly a decade after the Navy had appeared. The funny thing was that the Colt Navy Model 1851 hadn't come out in 1851 like you'd figure. For that matter, neither had the Pocket Model 1849 Dragoon. Colt had conceived of both weapons in 1847 when his Walker Colts were coming off the assembly line at Whitneyville. But I reckon he had learned a lesson from the way he had marketed his first pistol, the Paterson, and had decided to get as much promotion and coverage for each pistol he brought out from then on as he could. The Dragoon pistol that James carried with him now came out shortly after the Walker. Most people figure that a gun comes out in the year of the model it's given, but both the Baby Dragoon and the Navy came out in 1850!

If marketing was what was keeping Sam Colt in his firearms business, well, hoss, I reckon he made a smart move by bringing those guns out when he did. The Dragoon was now the official pistol of the US Army, and Sam Colt had sold over one hundred thousand of the model to both the government and private individuals since it had come out. The only other weapon giving it a run for its money for popularity was the Navy, though in a way that was sort of hard to believe.

The Navy came in .36 caliber with a seven-and-a-half-inch barrel but weighed just over two and a half pounds, making it far lighter than the .44 Dragoon. Colt had developed it for the Navy, hence its name, but it was the government in general that had contracted for them in 1855, sending them out every which way. The pistol grip had a comfortable fit to your hand, along with a squared-back trigger guard. The cylinder carried six shots, like every pistol Colt had made since the Walker, and just taking a gander at the engraving on the cylinder was enough to give you an idea of what Sam Colt thought of the Texas Navy if not the US Navy. The engraving depicted a naval engagement and was dated May 16, 1843. Whether you've heard of it or not, that was what became known as the battle of Campeche, a naval fight the Texicans won over the Mexicans and one for which they gave thanks to Sam Colt's Paterson pistols.

The gun I had just been issued must have been a newer or different model of the Navy than my old Colts, for there were two differences in its looks. The trigger guard was rounded, and there was no engraving anywhere on it. It balanced out the same as my own model, so I knew it would be just as effective. Besides, us Callahans ain't much on fancifulness. Still, I found myself looking at the bigger gun, the Dragoon, that James carried and wondering if I'd not be better of with such a model as he had.

"Jim?"

"Yeah." He looked up from his cup, which he'd just refilled, and offered me some.

"You recall that buffalo we shot on the way

over here?" I knew he'd remember the incident, for he had thought it comical at the time. I had emptied my five .36-caliber ball slugs into a buffalo at fairly close range, trying to kill him, but had only made him mad until James pulled out his Dragoon, got as close to the old bull as he could, and shot him dead. In a way, I reckon you could say he had the same mentality about the .36 Navy as Nathan did. Both father and son had made it known that they thought you needed a bigger gun for a bigger country like this and considered anything less than a .44 to be inefficient.

"Yeah," he said with a smile.

"You really think this Navy'll be enough gun for the places I'll be going?" If there was doubt in my voice, it wasn't put on at all, for I wanted to live as much as the next man. And I reckon Jim caught hold of my line of thought.

"Don't you worry 'bout it, Sean, you'll do fine." When the frown didn't leave my face, he tried a new tack. "Listen, if you don't tell Pa, I'll tell you something he said to me when I left home."

"Really!" I tried not to sound like an excited kid, even though I really felt like one right then.

"Yup." Then he paused a moment, as though to gather his thoughts. "I reckon there's two things you got to remember that are important. If you're thinking on how your Navy didn't do in that buffalo, well, Sean, you've got to recall that that was one helluva thick-skinned animal we was tangling with. And ain't but one other human that's got skin thick as that, and that's Pa."

We both smiled at Jim's remark, knowing how many times Nathan Hale Callahan, his pa and my brother, had been shot and got up and still kept walking. Oh, he was tough all right, no doubt about that.

"What's the other?" I asked, trying to sound serious again.

"Well," he said, drawing it out as though he were once again arranging his thoughts. "I reckon the other is what Pa said. He said that it ain't what you've got, it's how you use it. So you make the best of that Navy you got, Sean, and if what Pa said was right, why, I figure you'll do right fine."

"Are you sure that's all he said?" I asked, seeing Jim start to blush some. It was the first time I'd seen him do that while he was smiling, and I got to wondering if there was something he hadn't told me. "Just about using guns and all?"

"Uh . . . yeah, Sean, guns. That was all he said, all he talked about. Just your gun." He was still smiling and still blushing some, too. And I was still wondering.

At times Jim could be a real puzzle. Yes, he could.

There were quarters for us who had hired on as Pony Express riders to stay at, so the next morning Jim and I headed over to them. He was helping me get settled in, when Wash Bernard came along and I introduced him to Jim. As he had done the day before, Wash simply grunted a mumbled hello and went on about his business.

"I know he seems kind of strange, Jim," I said as he gave me a sideward glance, "but believe it or not, I sort of like him."

"Tired or troubled, one," was all Jim would say, but I could tell he had taken a bit of an interest in the young lad too. When we were through, I saw Jim look around to see if he could spot Wash. Not that it was hard, since the quarters resembled that of an army barracks more than anything else, being open and all.

When he spotted Wash, Jim walked over to his area, exchanged words of some sort, and then waved me over.

"I asked your friend here if he'd like to go with us over to the saloon down the block," Jim said. "They got a lunch counter and sody of sorts from what I hear." He was looking at me, but it was Wash he was talking to.

"Sure," I said. "Want to go?" The way Wash glanced at me, I was beginning to wonder if what Jim had said earlier wasn't more than idle speculation, for the boy surely did seem to shy away from people. Finally, he shrugged and mumbled "I reckon," and we left.

Jim had a way about him, I'll say that much. It might only have been a block or so to where we were going, but Jim had that boy talking to him when we were only a few feet out of the building. Me, I just took my time, walking and listening to the two of them.

"I'll bet they's a lot of young'uns come here claiming to be orphans, like the sign says."

"Sure," Wash said, "but most of them ain't that at all."

There was a moment of silence as neither of them said a word. Then Jim spoke up in a softer tone of voice than he usually used.

"Except you?" It was sort of like he knew the kid had a secret to keep and didn't want to spread it around any more than Wash did.

"Yeah. I reckon." If it was possible to be shy and defiant at the same time, you could say Wash Bernard was doing his best to prove it. His voice might have sounded hard, but I could tell by the look on his face that he was trying too hard to be what he wasn't—tougher than nails. If he was orphaned, I was betting it was just recently, for the toughness he was putting forth, well, it just wasn't really there. The boy was obviously still hurting from something.

We were silent the short distance that was left of our walk, but I did a lot of thinking in that brief time. Mind you now, I never laid any claim to thinking being my long suit, for that was more what Finn was good at than me. But I made a decision just then. I had no idea whether the boy was from the city or the country, but what I did know was that he was going to have to be able to live up to his outwardly tough manner. And I knew well enough how hard things could be on a person when they hurt on the inside. So I reckon you could say I sort of adopted George Washington Bernard for as long as he and I were working together on the Pony. Maybe I could help him out some. Besides, Jim had talked about taking on responsibility, so I figured this ought to be a step in the right direction.

The saloon looked more permanent than most I had seen. Not that I had gotten to see that many. But even the false fronts were a way of life for many a liquor haven. The chairs and tables were put together well enough to sit in without breaking, but the bar was just a thick piece of wood that had been stretched across beer barrels. And unless the barrels were filled with dirt or sand or something, they didn't look as though they'd stand much hard leaning.

Jim was right about the lunch counter, and we stepped up to the door side of the bar as we entered, for that was where the small sandwiches were located. Once my eyes had adjusted to the darkness, I could see that business had not been brisk so far that day, there being only three or four others lined up at the bar. I didn't recognize any of them, although I had no reason to, since they were all older men. Jim ordered a beer for himself and inquired as to the kind of soda the barkeep had. He smiled at us when the man set two root beers in front of us.

"You know, it was back in '46 that I came

into my first bar in Saint Louis and seen my first good fight. I was drinking root beer then, too." I knew the story Jim was referring to but let him go on with it. Perhaps Wash would like it.

"Harry, I didn't know you was serving chillern," the man next to Jim said louder than necessary as Jim was telling his story.

"Mister, do you mind?" Jim said politely. He had his hat pushed back on his forehead some, and he reached up to push it back farther now. "I was just telling the boys a story, and you're mighty disruptive."

"Brought the circus to town with you, too, I see," the man said, ignoring Jim. I do believe Jim could have handled it all right, but Wash jumped out in front of the man, who had been eying our new red shirts and blue pants when he spoke.

"I ain't no clown, mister," Wash said, placing hands on hips as though he were some tough hombre his own self. "Don't you talk to me that way!"

"Don't sass me, boy," was all the man said before he backhanded Wash. I could almost feel the dull thud as his big, beefy hand landed up alongside Wash's head and the boy went reeling to the floor.

Jim was down at his side in an instant, patting Wash on the cheek to bring him to. A quick glance was all I needed to see that Jim was getting mad. But he was nothing like Nathan, nothing like his pa. Nathan would have lit into everyone in that saloon who gave him a hard time, no matter what. Jim, well, I reckon you could say he was different that way. He was Irish all right, but I got the feeling time and again that his was a slow burn. And for my money, hoss, that's the kind you've got to look out for, 'cause when they go off the whole keg explodes and there ain't no tellin where you *or* he are going to wind up!

There was a little trickle of blood coming down Wash's face as his cheek puffed up and Jim helped him to his feet. Apparently the bully had had his fun, for he had gone back to palavering with his friends now. And here was Jim, trying to make light of it all.

"I never did finish telling you about that fight, did I?" He smiled, but I knew he could feel the pain Wash was going through and didn't like it any more than I did.

"How did it end, Mr. Callahan?" The boy's

voice sounded lifeless, as though the grit had left him for good. Or maybe he was expecting too much too soon from both Jim and me.

"Strange that you should ask," Jim said. I didn't think Wash Bernard could spot it, but I knew good and well there was an edge to his voice now, an edge that told me what Jim was thinking. "It started just like this did, with some big, goofy-looking fella pushing me off'n my stool and onto the floor." Now it was Jim who spoke loud enough to be heard throughout the room. "That's when my pa and his brother commenced to taking these fellas apart like they was so much deadwood looking for a fire to feed."

Jim sipped his beer and glanced at the bully next to him, knowing the man had overheard him. I saw him too, and his face was turning beet red, and I knew he was just wanting to sass Jim again.

"Tut, tut!" Jim said, pleasant as could be, raising his hand to the man. "Got to finish the story, don't you know." Then he turned his back on the bully, totally ignoring him as he focused his gaze on the blood on Wash's cheek. He said nothing for the longest time and then took another sip of his beer. There had been a bit of the Irish brogue in his voice, the way he'd get once in a while when storytelling, but now it was gone.

"You know how you're always asking me, Sean, about the way I wear my hat? Why I'm always pushing it back on my head?"

Jim wasn't looking at me now, only staring straight ahead into what could be seen in the distance only by himself alone.

"Sure." I said it as calmly as I could, not knowing what he was up to.

"Well, I wear it back like that so I can see what's going on around me. Fact is, there's times I wonder if you can't tell a man by the way he wears his headgear, and there's one type I always suspect."

"What kind's that?"

Out of the corner of his eye he glanced at the bully next to him.

"Fellas that wear their hats right down on the bridge of their nose. Those are the shortsighted kind, for they can't see much further than their noses."

"But what's that got to do with—"

"What it comes down to, Sean," he said, a sternness in him now as he faced me, "is being your own man. You just remember two things."

At this point he glanced at Wash as he said, "Always stand by your friends." Then, looking at me, he added, "And don't back water from anyone."

The big man's friend had been talking to him while Jim said his piece and finished his beer. Then the two next to Jim gave a hard look our way, nestling their hands just a little too close to their pistols to make me feel comfortable.

"Did you say your name was Callahan?" the big one asked, and I thought I saw a bit of greed in his eye.

"Among other things, that's what I've been called." Jim knew as well as I what was going through that man's mind, and that was when I knew there was trouble coming. Looking at me, Jim repeated, "Never back water from anyone. Especially the ugly ones."

Then he tossed the beer glass to the bartender. It got everyone's attention, which was just what he needed, for it was then that he hit the big man, just as the man was going for his gun.

He hit him hard, and I thought something had busted, either Jim's knuckles or the man's jaw line. It was when the bully staggered back and Jim hit him a second time that I knew it was the big man who was hurting now. He fell flat on his back, unconscious, and didn't look so awful big anymore as Wash rushed to his side and pulled his pistol from his waistband, then backed off.

I never will know if Jim didn't see the fella who'd been palavering with the big one or if he was seeing what I'd do in a pinch. I never did have time to ask. It was a time for doing, and I did. Jim had stepped away from the bar when the second man, behind him, pulled out his knife. The man had his eye on Jim's back and would have shoved the knife in hilt deep if he had had the chance, but I didn't let him. He was bigger and stronger than me, and Jim was like a brother to me, and that was all I could think of as I moved toward him.

I kicked him square in his elsewheres, and he folded in half, letting out a groan. Jim turned as soon as he heard it, grabbed the man by the scalp, and flung his head back, landing three hard punches to his face before that man, too, sank to the floor.

The other two at the bar had backed off and either didn't know the ones who had started the fandango or didn't want any part of it.

"Don't you do it, mister, or I'll kill you. I swear I will!" The big one had come to and, noting that his pistol was gone, was in the process of reaching for his bowie, when Wash yelled out what he did. Both Jim and I turned to see the boy, scared enough to be a shaky specimen with that cocked pistol but also desperate enough to pull the trigger and carry out his threat.

The barkeep was going for something under the bar, and I was betting it wasn't a clean glass to offer us a refill on our drinks, for he was getting a fed-up look about him, too. That was when Jim stepped across the body of the man Wash was covering and pulled his Dragoon, pointing it straight at the barman as his hand half appeared from behind the bar. I did the best thing I knew, and that was to move to the side of the street entrance just in case some of these fellas had friends sympathetic to their cause, whatever that was.

"I never was much on scripture quoting, friend," Jim said, his hand as steady as a rock as he took aim at the barkeep, "but it seems to me that somewhere a fella said that a full house divided don't win no pots. Now, we can call it a draw and leave it like it is, or you can decide you don't like the Irish and we'll end everything right here and now. What'll it be?"

I think he was glad he had a choice, that barkeep, for he let go of whatever was in his hand right quick, as though someone had set fire to it. "Get out of here," was all he grumbled.

We didn't put our guns away until we were out on the street and on our way. But if one thing had been accomplished, it was the change in Wash's attitude. He was looking now as though he had actually accomplished something worthwhile.

"Are you sure that was the Bible you were quoting in there, Mr. Callahan?" the boy asked in a chipper mood.

"Call me Jim." We walked a bit before he spoke again, a touch of mischief about him. "And that wasn't the Good Book exactly that I was quoting."

"Then what was it?"

"Well," Jim said, that reckless smile on his face now, "I call it the gospel according to Callahan."

"Sir?" Wash had a genuine expression of bewilderment on his face.

But Jim only smiled.

"I can see I'm going to have to teach you lads how to play poker."

4

I WAS only half watching Jim do a patch-up job on Wash Bernard's cheek. I reckon I was more concerned with the door to our quarters and the inevitable visit from one of the supervisors about the ruckus in the saloon. Such gossip spread like wildfire, and the only thing running through my mind right now was staying in good standing with the people running this operation; that meant living up to my end of the bargain I'd made with them when I signed that oath about not fighting with fellow employees.

"That ought to do you up," Jim was saying, finishing his doctor work on Wash as the door opened. It was Buckmaster who filled the wide space, taking in the occupants of the barrack as he adjusted his eyes to the lesser light. He was dressed as when I had first seen him the day before, wearing his black broadcloth and Quaker hat.

"I understand there was a difficulty," he said to no particular one of the three of us as he approached my bunk. "Over at the saloon, if what I'm told is correct." He cocked an eyebrow at me, an apparent dare to deny his statement.

"You heard right, Mr. Buckmaster." I stood up as I said it. The man towered over me, but standing my ground brought me that much closer to him, and I never was one to have people talking down at me.

"Would you care to explain it?" He was nothing like the two rowdies we had run into at the bar, for although his voice was firm, it bore none of the pushiness of the other men.

"Actually, Mr. Buckmaster, there ain't an awful lot to explain." It was Jim again, hat pushed back on his head, stepping in to take care of things. "You see, I took these lads over there to get a swish of something cool, and, well"—here he shrugged—"it seems these two fellas was on the prod and decided to pick a fight with Mr. Bernard here." He nodded toward Wash, but I could see that the boy had forgotten all about the patch on his face and was taken with the excitement of being addressed as "mister".

"Mind you, now, Mr. Buckmaster, I done read that oath the boys had to sign, that one about not fighting and all. And I figured they deserve a chance to prove themselves a-riding for your Pony Express."

"I see." I could tell Buckmaster only half believed what Jim was saying.

"So when the ugly one drew blood on Wash, here," Jim continued, "why, I just stepped in and finished the ball, me not being one of your employees and all. Not that I don't figure these lads couldn't take care of their own selves, you understand. Nosiree, they'd do right fine." With that lazy grin on his face, he winked at us.

"I understand there was almost some gunplay, too."

"Almost," Wash said with more confidence than I'd heard him express so far. "I picked up that one fella's pistol after Mr. Callahan knocked him down. Didn't want him to get accidentally shot or anything." He was as calm as could be now, and I found myself wondering if it might not be out of pure desperation at the thought of losing a job even before he'd started it.

"And you?" he said, giving me an equally hard look. "I heard your pistol was out of its holster, too."

"I was checking my loads," I said in dead earnest. "A body never can tell when he's going to need his guns."

"Well, gentlemen," he said, giving us all a scrutinizing glance, "my grandmother would have called your stories pure bunk. And believe me, if it weren't that Mr. Majors doesn't care for profanity, I'd use some awfully strong terms to tell you just what I think of this whole business. As it is, you boys can consider yourselves on good behavior, because if this happens just *one more time* . . ." His voice trailed off, and all he did now was shake his head back and forth at us very slowly. The message, although unspoken, was clear enough.

He headed back toward the entrance and then stopped briefly before facing us again.

"And Mr. Callahan?" There was no mistaking the fact that he was talking to Jim instead of me.

"Yes?"

"The next time you get an urge to take your drinks in the saloon, I would appreciate it if you'd do it alone." Again, there was a certain amount of respect in his voice as he spoke, with his statement sounding more like a personal favor than a command.

Jim smiled and nodded. "We understand each other."

It was two weeks until our first run was to be made on April 3, 1860. During that time the supervisors like Buckmaster made good their promise to see which of us could handle a horse well enough to serve as riders. There seemed to be a mountain of chores that needed doing from can see to can't see, but it was just as well we got used to them, for as the man had said, when we weren't riding and had time on our hands, we would be expected to chip in and help out around our various stations.

Yet there was much excitement about the starting of the Pony, as it was being called, and the community in general was more than pleased to entertain those of us who had signed up. During that two weeks' time there was a number of dances for those who had a lady friend to take or who wanted to meet a lady or two; that was more in Jim's line than mine. Like I said, the only stockings I was interested in were the ones on the mounts I would have for my rides. So while Jim was looking over the ladies, most of the boys my age and I were racing horses and engaging in the other games set up for our benefit.

In what little idle time I did have, I took to wondering where Jim would go from here and what he would do. I knew that I would be going somewhere west of here on an adventure I was looking forward to. But what about Jim? Would he go back to drifting, to doing a job here and there? Or what? I couldn't picture him doing anything else, until one night when he dragged me along to one of the dances. I was dead set against going, but as much as I loved the horse racing, I wanted to stay in Jim's good graces. So I went. And that was the night I learned what Jim had in mind not too far down the road.

I stood at the punch bowl trying to avoid the looks of some of the young girls who couldn't have been much older than me, when Jim disappeared in the crowd and then returned with a woman on his arm.

"Sean, I want you to meet Alicia." The way he said it, you'd think it was the proudest thing he'd ever done, introducing us. "Alicia, this is my . . . kin, Sean. He's riding for the Pony."

"How do, ma'am," I said. Nervous as I was, I grabbed my hat by the front and yanked it off before sticking out a hand to meet hers. I reckon that's the way you are at that age, but I do recall that the palm of my hand was sweaty as it touched hers. I felt like I'd catch some kind of disease if I held her hand too long, and so I let go of it right quick.

"Why don't you two talk," Jim said. "I got to get some more fixings for this punch bowl before the well goes dry." I got the feeling that Jim was almost as nervous about me meeting this girl as I was.

When Jim was gone, we stood there for a few silent moments taking each other in. Me, I knew I wasn't much to look at but a gangly fourteen-year-old, but this girl, this woman, well, hoss, Jim could pick them, that he could. She had brown hair that hung well past her shoulders, with eyes to match her hair. There were dimples in her cheeks when she smiled, like she was doing now, and it gave me the notion that she was a pleasant young lady to be with. Maybe a few years older than me, but just as many years younger than Jim. I had heard talk about some of the hard, shiftless women who showed up on the frontier, but this wasn't one of them. She wasn't all that tall, and for some strange reason I didn't even think of that cruel joke that had been played on me down in Santa Fe the year before, as I usually did when I came across a girl or a young woman. Fact is, to look at her you'd think she was pure innocence all packaged up in a fancy dress.

"If you keep rolling your hat in your fist like that," she said, "the brim will never flatten out."

"Oh. Well, ma'am, it's something I'm working on." I wasn't sure just what else to say, but it didn't seem to matter, for she made no nevermind about it. Just to have something to do, I got us both some of the dwindling supply of punch, and by that time Jim had returned with a refill for the bowl. I reckon he knew how awkward I was feeling right then, for he started conversing while he was pouring the punch.

"You know, this ain't the first time an outfit like the Pony Express has come along." Alicia must not have figured Jim for any more the book-learning type than I had, and she looked as surprised at the authority with which he spoke as I did.

"Really?" Alicia was taking a real interest in what Jim was saying, but between you and me, friend, I got the idea that she'd get interested in his line of thought even if it drifted to buffalo chips, the way she was looking at him.

"You sure?" Me, I had some doubts about what he was talking about. After all, who wanted to be part of a second-string outfit?

"Sure," Jim said, setting the container down and moving around to the front of the table. "Fella name of Darius, about four centuries back, they say he had the best courier system in the East. Run just like the Pony Express is aiming to, from what I understand."

"But how can that be?" I asked, now thoroughly confused at what he was saying. Darius? I'd never heard of the man. The East? Why that was pure . . . "Jim, you're joshing me, ain't you? The East is back yonder," I said, throwing a thumb over my shoulder.

"I think what Jim is speaking of is a land called Persia where Darius ruled." She was smart, this girl, and not pushy about it either, for she simply smiled at me when she spoke. Like I said, most all of the people in the community were making us feel welcome.

"Yeah, that's the place." Jim seemed to be excited about the subject again now that he was back on the right track. "That's what Finn was saying." Then, to Alicia, he added, "Finn, he's the book reader in the family."

"Oh?" She seemed pretty impressed, and I wondered if she might be a schoolteacher in the making. "Did he ever tell you about the adventures of Marco Polo?"

"He surely did, Alicia, he surely did." He got himself a cup of the punch and proceeded to scratch the back of his head with his free hand. "But I reckon I'm kind of slow some ways. You see, once you get me east of the Mississippi or out onto that Pacific Ocean, why I couldn't tell you direction worth spit."

"I don't understand." And if she didn't, I reckon I didn't either, for I'd always thought Jim to be right smart.

"Well, I asked Finn about Marco Polo and this Darius fella and where they lived," he said sheepishly, "and Finn said out across the Pacific."

"But why would that be a problem?"

"Why, Alicia, he said they lived in the East, and just like Sean here, I asked him how could that be. And Finn, well, he just kept pointing west and said they was so far west, they called it east where these fellas lived. I never will figure that one out," he said, still scratching his head.

But it made the girl laugh, and I reckon that's what those dances and parties were for. And like I said, it was that night I figured out what Jim would likely be doing with himself once I started working the Pony. You see, he and Alicia took to dancing, and I sort of guarded the punch bowl while they did those lively steps. But it was seeing the way they were looking at each other that told me what I wasn't sure I wanted to know.

Jim's pa, Nathan; why, I reckon I got raised as much by him as Jim did, and I had no regrets about it. I learned a lot of things from him, and one was that you could tell a lot about what was going on inside a man's mind by the look in his eyes. Now, I wasn't too awful crazy about girls and women and such, you understand, but I'd seen the same look about Nathan and Finn when they had a certain yearning for their wives, and I remembered it that night. For Jim and Alicia had that same look.

To tell the truth, I think they were in love.

5

THOSE two weeks went pretty fast. By the time the first Pony rider was to catch saddle and ride came around, the hundred and some who had signed up didn't exist anymore. Our ranks had been thinned quite a bit and there would be only eighty riders to start out with. The idea was that forty of them would be going east and another forty west, at the same time delivering the mail in both directions. Not all the riders had been chosen there in Saint Joe, for there were supervisors and station managers farther west who had picked riders from their own territory. Those boys would likely ride their own territory and serve in the terrain they knew fairly well. Me, I think I sort of confused them all when I said I was from all over and would ride wherever they put me. Wash Bernard did the same, and we got teamed up that way, probably because we got along so well.

Buckmaster had talked to Jim not long before the first ride was to be made and worked out a deal in which Jim would be hired on to do general troubleshooting and wrangling duties. I figured he took Jim on because of the way he'd handled the two toughs in the saloon more than anything. And to tell the truth, I don't think Jim would have taken the job had it not been for Alicia's father heading west to serve as home station manager on the route and taking her with him. Aaron Stiles was a big man who would double as a blacksmith, the kind of man you'd naturally not want to tangle with. But I don't think I'd ever seen anyone gentler around Alicia than her father, unless it was Jim.

Jim's first duty would be to drive a remuda of horses out to one of the home stations and make sure all went well in the operation of that station. Orders for other jobs by him would be sent along in messages from Saint Joe. He was in a cheerful mood when he left a few days before the first run, but I reckon I couldn't blame him, for Alicia and her father were accompanying him.

Jim had been gone a few days, and it wasn't but a day or two until the first ride when Wash and I were making ready to leave for the stations we'd be riding from. We were saddling up the horses at our livery when they cornered us.

"Where's your friend?" It was the big, ugly one who had started it all in the saloon who spoke. I noticed that he was missing a tooth and that he spoke with a bit of a lisp because of it. His partner was with him.

"He's gone," I said, feeling scared as hell but wanting not to show it. "Why, you going to start something again?"

"Just finish it, boy." He started to take a step toward me, when Wash's mount whinnied as though it had been spooked. The man took an immediate step to the rear, turning his attention to Wash. "What'd you do, boy?" he said angrily.

But Wash just sort of smiled, almost as if he were imitating Jim in his careless manner.

"'Tain't me, mister," he said, "it's you. Do you smell that bad to everyone who gets a wind of the south side of you?"

"Why, you little whelp!" He said it as he was making his way around the back end of Wash's horse, and he was plenty loud in saying it, which he shouldn't have been.

"Callahan? Bernard?" I heard a familiar voice outside the entrance to the livery as Buckmaster came into view, as big as ever, and everyone sort of took notice. He was that kind of man. "I heard a horse. Is there a problem?" He said it as casual as could be, but all of us knew it didn't take a fool to see what was about to happen. I guessed then that Wash had gotten his horse to rear up on purpose to get the supervisor's attention. Otherwise we'd have been gone beaver.

"Nothing to concern you," the plug-ugly said, and continued his stalk toward Wash. He got past the horse's rump, and I couldn't see anything from there on. I only heard him yell and cuss when Wash kicked him somewhere, but that only lasted for a second or two before I saw his hand come up over the back of the horse. He was getting ready to slap Wash just as he had in the saloon.

Except he never did.

Buckmaster had been walking ever since he entered the livery, even while he was speaking, and he didn't stop until he caught the big man's arm on my side of the horse and pulled it back far enough to swing him around. When he let go, he brought one of his hamlike fists across the side of the ruffian's face, knocking the man backwards in a staggering motion. But Buckmaster didn't stop there. He hit the man full in the face again as he tried to regain his balance, only to slip on some manure and fall again to the floor after being hit.

Meanwhile, his friend was thinking on an easier way to get rid of his problems. His hand was on the butt of his pistol, but I had mine out and trained right on his chest at full cock. And I don't mind telling you I was scared as hell and don't doubt that it showed in what I said.

"Mister," I said in a half yell to make sure I got his attention, beads of sweat breaking out on my forehead. Maybe it was the cocking of the pistol that made him turn my way, but when he did, I spoke my piece. "I ain't never killed a man before, but I'll tell you right now that if you make me much more nervous . . . well, I'm going to shoot you."

He was studying on it. I could see that much in his eyes as he gave me the hardest stare I'd ever come across. I don't think he was any more certain I'd shoot than I was at that moment. But when his grip tightened on his pistol, a chill went down my spine, and I knew he was going to try to take me.

Except he didn't.

"And after he shoots you, I will too!" I don't know which was louder, Wash's voice or the sound of that rifle he was cocking. But it sure enough got the fella's attention. Right quick.

"They sound pretty determined," Buckmaster said. Apparently, he had taken the pistol from the now unconscious man beside him. Three guns was too much, even for the man before us, and he loosened his grip, letting his hand fall to his side. "I knew that'd bring you around," Buckmaster said with a smile. "Rodell and Hardin, isn't it?"

"What about it?" the other man said, losing none of the toughness in his voice.

"The sheriff is a good friend of mine. I'm sure he'd like to have a conversation with you and your friend about how to conduct yourself in our town."

"Not as much as he'd like to talk to him," he replied, nodding toward me. "He's wanted, him and his friend."

A brief frown crossed Buckmaster's face as he glanced at me and then back to the ruffian.

"The only place Mr. Callahan is wanted is right here by me. He and Mr. Bernard work for me, and you'll do well to stay away from them. They have more important matters to attend to." Then he pulled the gun from the man's holster, hefting both it and the still unconscious man's pistol in his fists. "You can pick these up at the sheriff's office in about an hour . . . on your way *out of town*." Buckmaster said this last part through gritted teeth, so there was no doubt that he meant it. "Now get your friend out of here. I have enough manure to clean up without having to take care of him."

Rodell or Hardin, whoever he was, sort of got red in the face as Wash and I chuckled at Buckmaster's comment. It was the kind of thing I wanted to say but could never have thought of in time.

When the two plug-uglies had left, Buckmaster turned to me with a curious look on his face. "Is that true, what he said about you being wanted?"

"I don't know," I said, putting away my Navy pistol. "I heard talk, but neither Jim nor I have seen anyone come after us."

"Run-in with the law?" For running an outfit that seemed to hold pretty high moral standards, the man didn't seem too awful concerned with my past.

"Sorta. The disagreement's more on who started it than anything else."

He smiled the way a friend does when you're explaining your problems to him. "That's usually the way of it. But enough of that. You two have a ride to get ready for as I recall."

"Thanks for stepping in, Mr. Buckmaster," Wash said as the supervisor was leaving. "I reckon if you hadn't come along, those two woulda done us in good."

He smiled again. "All part of the job." Then he left, heading for the sheriff's office. Watching him go set me to thinking, and by the time we had those horses ready to set out for our stations I pretty much looked the way I felt.

"What's the matter, Sean?" Wash asked as we headed out of town. "You look like you could fight a grizzly bear."

"Reckon I could," I said, my frown getting deeper.

We rode a ways in silence. The town was just about on the horizon before Wash pulled to a halt.

"What's eatin' you, Sean?" I had the impression he wanted me to get it out in the open as much as I did, so I spoke my mind.

"I'm just tired of being looked after, Wash." He seemed a bit confused at what I said. "It's the fight in the saloon . . . and the one just now back there."

"What about 'em?"

"Well, don't you see, each time we got twixt a rock and a hard place, why, there was someone there to step in and take over. Not that I don't appreciate what Jim or Mr. Buckmaster did for us, but if we got to take care of our own selves, well—"

"We ought to take care of our own selves," Wash finished my thought. "Yeah, I know what you mean, Sean. That's why I've been looking for the day we could be out on our own."

"But those two back there," I said, still disappointed at my lack of action. "Rodell and Hardin—"

"Oh, we ain't seen the last of them." Suddenly, there was a look on his face that was a combination of fear and excitement, as strange as that may seem.

"How's that?"

"When Buckmaster was talking to you, the one that he took a fist to woke up and told me he'd foller us, said that one day we'd be looking up and there he'd be and that would be that!"

There was a moment of silence before he spoke again. "You think he meant it, Sean?"

I shrugged. "Hard telling. My older brother told me once that men who make threats like that are mostly blowhards bitter about the world and too damn lazy to change anything, so they complain about it." I said a silent prayer that for once I was right, for what Wash had said didn't make our lifes sound much like they were worth anything but a bounty.

"You sure?"

He was scared now, the bravado gone from him. Here I had started out telling him what was ailing me, and now I had him worried all to hell and gone. Then I remembered how I'd made that decision to do what I could for Wash Bernard, along with what Jim had said about standing by your friends. Well, I reckon there wasn't much else I could say but what I did.

"Yeah, I'm sure, Wash. And even if he does come after us, even if *they* come after us, we'll be ready."

"But how are we going to do that?"

"What we don't learn from others, we'll teach ourselves, *pard*." I emphasized that last word as though we were both men, both saddle pards. Then I tried to smile the way I thought

Jim would when I said, "Besides, by then I figure we'll be tougher'n nails. Now what say we light a shuck?"

And that we did. I do believe it sort of boosted Wash's morale to hear that, I really do. And me? Well, hoss, inside I was praying real hard that I'd be able to live up to my own prediction.

6

IT couldn't have been more than four feet deep, and how the fella running the place survived I'll never know. Hell, it wasn't even a sod dugout like some I'd run across earlier. What did he do when winter came?

"Lemme have that mount," he said as I slid off and began to transfer the mochila to the ready mount. "No, no," he said, placing a skinny arm on my shoulder. "I'll get that. You go to the fire and get yourself some coffee and help yourself to what's left of my meal."

One glance at him, the horse, and the food by the fire and I opted for the food. Maybe that was how he stayed so skinny, giving away his meals. It couldn't have been for lack of appetite, for the stuff tasted damn good! But then I reckon it could have had a tincture of buffalo chip in it and I'd still have thought it tasted fine. You do that when you're hungry and don't eat regular, I was finding out.

It was my first week as a rider, and although it hadn't been all that dangerous so far, the riding that I used to take so much pleasure in was turning out to be a real test of durability for both the riders of the Pony and their mounts.

I'd seen half a dozen shacks that looked better than this fella's, but somehow it didn't matter, for as long as he could have the relay horses ready on time, well, I reckon he was keeping up his end of the bargain and so be it.

My two minutes were about up as I tossed aside the empty plate and coffee cup and headed for a fresh mount. I didn't mind the red shirt and blue pants we riders had to wear, although in some of the country I passed through they seemed an almighty easy target for someone who might want to stop me. And so far I'd managed to hide the fact that rather than carry just the one issue of the Colt Navy I was wearing a brace of them, mine where I always did and the new one as a backup on my right hip. What was bothersome was this horn they wanted me to blow before I came upon my next station. At most of the relay stations they said they could hear me coming in the distance anyway, so I figured the horn was just one more piece of useless material I had to carry.

"Good time so far, son." Like a lot of the men who worked the relays, he was older than I, maybe pushing thirty, I couldn't tell. It made me wonder at times if us young ones hadn't been hired just to hold on to a pair of reins and take our chances, for the horses seemed to have a sense of their own and knew the trails we were following almost better than us riders. A man, especially a lone man, who worked a relay had to rely on his wits in case he got between a rock and a hard spot, and the men doing those jobs all seemed like seasoned frontiersmen. So it gave a body a chance to wonder.

In what little time I had, that was, and right now I had no time.

"What do you think of souvenirs, friend?" I asked, climbing into the saddle.

"Well, I reckon that depends on what they is."

"You musically inclined?"

He shrugged and smiled. "Pick a banjo when I get a chance."

"Well, mister, you just got another instrument you can learn to play," I said, taking off the cumbersome horn. "This thing plays hell on my side with all the jostling around I do, so you can have it. And if anyone asks you, just tell 'em you're hanging on to it for safekeeping for me."

I didn't know if he was surprised that I'd give up a part of my issue or if it was my making a present of it to him that had struck him, but he didn't seem to object much.

"All right, son, I'll do that." He smiled again.

"By the way, my ma always said to tell a good cook about it when they set a fine table."

This seemed to surprise him even more, and he raised an eyebrow.

"That so?"

"And I'll tell you, mister, I don't see a table in sight, but the fixings at your fire are downright good."

"Why, thank you, son." Then he gave my mount a swat on the rump and yelled "Godspeed" to me, and I was gone.

That first month went by right fast. I didn't get much sleep, but I learned the trails, made a few extra rides for riders who got sick, and pulled what I figured was more than my share of the work load when I wasn't riding. I reckon that was the responsibility Jim had mentioned earlier.

So far the Pony had been on time, give or take a few hours, but never more then ten days from Saint Joe to Sacramento. I hadn't seen Wash Bernard in all that time either, but I figured he was holding his own on the trail as no one had mentioned different.

The riding and being outdoors were fine, but I reckon that for someone my age, hell, for *all* of us eighty riders, the word "adventure" meant danger, and so far there simply hadn't been any. But I didn't have to wait long, for in May word was put out that the Paiutes had gone on the warpath. And if the word was correct, any part of the trail through Utah, Nevada, and the Colorado Territories might hold a Paiute war party behind any turn in the route.

I had finagled what you might call an illegal transfer to the route a bit farther west. Jim must have been making quite a name for himself out in that region, for there were stories here and there about him and his troubleshooting. There were all sorts of excuses I could make up for going out there, but hell, the truth was he was family and I flat out missed him. Besides, he may have liked that girl, Alicia, but I had taken a liking to her pa. The one short time I had met Mr. Stiles struck me with what you'd call a good impression, I reckon, and it stuck with me.

The Kansas Territory had been right flat, but this land I was going to be traversing on my route was a bit more rolling in places and a damn sight prettier. Not that I had all that much time to take a gander at the scenery, you understand.

The home stations were located about seventy-five miles apart, with relays in between about fifteen miles apart. That was what Russell, Majors, and Waddell figured was safe riding for a horse without running him to death. Each of us had a fresh horse every fifteen miles, and the home station serviced the relays in the area. It had a blacksmith and extra horses in case a relay station ran short or had some mounts stolen by horse thieves or Indians. The home stations I'd be operating between were run by Alicia and her father on the east end and a fella who called himself "Captain" Jack Slade on the west end.

Slade wasn't any bigger than me, although a bit thicker in the chest and shoulders, but on that first meeting with him I didn't think I'd ever come across anyone who acted more like a decent person unless it was my own family. He explained the route to me as he readied the mount for my ride and we waited for the westbound rider to appear over the ridge.

"You keep your wits about you, son. Can't blame these Paiutes for getting hostile against whites, you know."

"Sir?"

"'Carse." He said it as if he were talking to a pilgrim who didn't know much of anything, and I reckon I didn't. "Look, what would you do if someone were to come in and shoot up your kin?"

"Reckon I'd go after 'em."

"That's right. And justified you'd be, too. And that's just how the Indians feel out here about the white man coming into their land and killing off their own." He paused a moment in thought before continuing. "What I'm saying, Callahan, is you see if you can't outdistance those red devils afore you figure to make a hero out of yourself by sending a few more of 'em to the happy hunting grounds. Your mission's to get the mail through."

"Yes, sir. I know."

He seemed like the kind of man a body could take a liking to if he chose. At least right then he did.

It was past noon when I rode into the fourth relay station. So far the trip had been uneventful, the riding not all that difficult. It was hearing that eastbound rider as he arrived at the same time I did that set my blood to stirring.

"Watch it back yonder," he said, as out of breath as his horse as he dismounted and switched his mochila to a fresh mount. I did the same as he went on. "They's Injuns on the hunt, and they ain't out to shake your hand and see you smile, hoss."

"Thanks. I'll keep an eye out."

He was gone before either of us could say anything else.

The eastbound rider was right, for halfway through my run I came on a clearing that wasn't forty yards ahead of me when I rounded the corner, and there they were! A war party of maybe fifteen or twenty braves just a-blocking my path like it wasn't there.

Now, I'll tell you, friend, I got more than a bit confused right then. Hell, I was downright scared and I'll admit it! The only thing going through my mind was how Slade had said to keep out of a fight and get the mail through

. . . and how much I didn't want to die! To tell the truth, I'd rather have been going up against those two hard cases back in Saint Joe all by my lonesome and dying at their hands than tackling these fellas. But I had taken an oath, and a man's got to keep his word, that's how I was brought up. So I made my decision not a split second after I rounded that bend and saw the war party.

I stuck the reins into my mouth and prayed to hell I didn't lose my teeth while I pulled out my two Navys and dug my heels into my mount. They had lances and bows and arrows and even a few rifles, likely taken off some whites they'd done in. But they didn't fire, and neither did I. I kept that horse a-running flat at them and held those Navys in plain sight so they'd know I was ready to open the ball if they wanted to dance. And I'll tell you, hoss, that was the loneliest silence I ever went through in my lifetime! Oh, there were my horse's hooves beating the ground, but I couldn't hear them, not at all. All I was listening for was that first shot from one of their rifles; all I was waiting to feel was one of their lances running right through my side and carrying me off my horse. How I made it that forty yards I'll never know.

At the last second they broke!

They didn't move until just five yards before I came on them. Then they broke ranks, and I found myself riding right through them, close enough to touch!

And not a shot was fired!

The only thing I could figure was that they were as confused and scared as I was. I'd heard that Indians didn't want nothing to do with crazy men, and after what I'd just done I was sure I must fall into that category. I only looked back once, and they were still sitting there, just watching me go.

Fact is, I was so scared, I still had those reins in my mouth and the Navys in my hand when I rode into the last relay station!

"If you're trying to impress someone, it'll never work," a voice said as my horse came to a halt. "On the other hand, if you've gone that long without food, I don't blame you."

I do believe that the only reason those reins came out of my mouth was because it fell open at the sight of Jim standing there before me, cockeyed grin and all.

"Well, you going to get down or not?"

It took me a second to recall the events that

had just happened, and then I tucked away the Navys and dismounted.

"Hey, you all right?" The smile was gone from his face now, replaced by a look of concern. When I realized my hands were shaking, I knew why.

Whoever it was that ran the station pushed a plateful of beans and a cup of coffee into my hands as I sat down and told Jim what I had just done.

"I'm proud of you, Sean," he said, slapping me on the back when I'd finished both the quick meal and the story. My hands had slowed down some but still held a little twitch to them.

"What are you doing here?" I asked him.

"Oh, just chasing some strays that got out of the corrals." There was only a second or two of silence before he went on, but after my confrontation with those Indians, I didn't think even one second of silence would ever be short again. Not a one. "You think you can make it to the home station?" he asked, all serious again.

I looked down at my hands and saw them still shaking.

"I gits that way, too," the old station manager said. "Don't get a proper meal in a long time, and I gits the shakes something fierce. Unnervy, it is."

"He's right," Jim said, but somehow I thought his smile was a bit overworked this time. "Just a lack of food, is all."

Was it, really? Or were they simply making light of the fact that I was scared to death and didn't want to admit it?

I went over to the horse and mounted up, with Jim following me.

"You know, Sean, any man who's gone through what you have is going to be plenty scared. And if he's smart, he'll confess it . . . to himself if nobody else. I reckon the important thing to remember is that it don't make you any less of a man to admit it."

"Yeah."

If I said it halfheartedly, well, I reckon that's the way I was feeling. I was riding out because it was part of the job, and I'd said I'd make it to the end.

I just wasn't too awful sure if I'd make it to the end of the ride or to my own end of the permanent type right around the corner and up ahead.

My horse wasn't the only thing that was moving

like lightning that last leg of the route. My mind was going a mile a minute, too. And all that was going through it was questions I had no answers to. Were there more Indians up ahead? Were the Paiutes that mad that they'd kill every white they came across? And if they were, did I have the guts to take them on, to fight like a man ought to? Did I really want manhood and all the responsibilities that went with it? All the hardships? All the *death*? Or was my need to make this ride simply a childish dream of someone who was between hay and grass and wasn't sure what he wanted? Why, when I wanted to do so well, to be so good at whatever it was I did, why did I feel like such a failure?

Some questions never get answered. Then there's some that, well, I reckon they sort of answer themselves, if you know what I mean. And some of these questions I was asking myself got answers on that last ride of my route.

There were stands of pinion I rode by that I was sure my mount would enjoy nuzzling up to if he had the chance; I knew I'd enjoy their shade if I had my druthers, too. Then there were rocky areas, pieces of flat land bordered by abutments of thick rock that made it almighty easy for a body to hide behind. I was coming up on one of those abutments when it happened.

They were Paiutes all right, same as that last bunch I'd had a run-in with. And it seemed there were a couple of dozen. All I knew was they were there and so was I, and they were pulling a flanking movement like I had never seen before! They came out from behind that huge rock formation on my right just like soldiers drilling on a parade field. They were flanking to their left and bringing a whole wedge of warriors out in front of me in the process, a movement that looked to be about two deep in riders.

And these fellas didn't waste no time in letting me know I wasn't welcome in their land, either. I'd only spotted one or two rifles, the rest being armed with lances and bows and arrows, as had the previous group of Paiutes. But as soon as they came into sight, they let fly those arrows, and I knew my end wasn't too far in the offing. By God, they were out for blood, and it was mine they were after!

Strange things happen to your mind when you get in a tight spot like that. One minute I figured my goose was cooked and I might as well throw the key in the bucket and chuck it down the well, and the next it was crossing my mind how badly I wanted to set a good example for Wash Bernard so I could give him the confidence I knew he needed. That all ran through my thoughts in one split second. I was reaching for my Navy, when the arrow hit me high in the left shoulder, knocking me out of the saddle.

I must have landed like a sack of grain on the hard rock ground, because I remember my bottom left cheek hurting more than my shoulder was.

And I got mad.

All of a sudden I was tired of being pushed around and babied and lectured to and Lord knows what else. Damn it, I was mad! Maybe that ain't the right Christian attitude to have when you know you're going to die, but I recalled something Nathan had said to me after he'd told one of his stories about fighting off the Comanch' when he was getting Ellie and James back from them some years back. "If you're going under and you know it, boy," he had said, "leave 'em a calling card. Let 'em know who it is they're burying." Until just then I wasn't sure what he had meant, but now I did. That arrow had put a lot of pain into my left side, and about all I could do with my left hand was pull out the other Colt pistol.

Some of the Paiutes had taken after my mount, and the rest were converging on me as I sat flat on my ass out in the open, waiting for them to get within pistol range. And as they did, only one thought ran through my mind and that was to hell with Alexander Majors and his oath, I had a few of my own!

"Sonsabitches!" I yelled out as loud as I could when they came at me. There were arrows flying everywhere, it seemed, and a lance landed near my side, spewing some dirt up to the side of my face, but I brushed it off and kept on yelling. "I may be scared, but I ain't afraid to die!" I yelled it twice while I was waiting for them to get in range, and then I knew it wouldn't do no good anyway.

I fired five times, and four of them were hits, right dead center in the group. Their horses ran past me and blocked the rest of the braves' aim until the dust cleared and they came at me again, and I did the same thing, only this time I hit five of them.

A tomahawk zipped past my shoulder, only the handle of it striking me, but another arrow found a mark in my thigh, and I was feeling more pain. I figured that was it and was setting down the Colt to draw my bowie, when I remembered that I'd fired only five shots. Quickly I found the extra shot left in each cylinder and put a cap on it and spun it to the right just so. One warrior, knife in hand, was ready to jump me from his pony, when I shot him and he landed with a thud right next to me. I only had one bullet left, and Nathan's words came running through my mind again. "Leave 'em a calling card."

"I'm Callahan, God damn you!" I yelled, firing the last shot, not even sure if I'd hit my mark and for that matter not even caring. What was important now was that they *know*. I put down the Navy and took up the bowie. "Callahan, you hear!"

"Betcherass!" was the faint echo that I heard as a distant gun began to boom and the remaining warriors began to disappear.

Some were dropping like flies!

The rest scattered here and there, those on horseback fleeing as fast as they could. The sound of the guns was getting closer. They were coming from the rear, and when I looked over my shoulder, I couldn't believe what I saw. Or maybe I should have expected it. There was Jim on his horse, guns in his hands, reins in his teeth, firing off those big Dragoons he carried. It seemed like an hour from start to finish, but it couldn't have taken more than a minute or so for it all to happen.

"Ain't had a decent meal lately?" I asked when he rode up and spit out the reins. I was feeling kind of light-headed, having just taken notice of the blood that was coming out of me.

"How you doing?" was all he said as he put away his guns and pulled off his neckerchief, tearing open my blue pants and placing it next to the wound. Then he got out his bowie and hacked off the necks of the arrows in me and gave me some water.

"You're going to have to hold on to me, Sean," he said, replacing my guns in their holsters and prying the bowie from my grip. "Can you do that?"

"Sure," I said. I had the feeling my voice was soft as I spoke, for he frowned at me as I looked about. There were dead Paiutes all over the place and a pool of blood where I had been sitting. I thought I saw Jim reloading one of his Dragoons before we got on his horse. Then I reached around from his back, grabbed hold of his belt in front, and held on for dear life.

The next thing I knew, we had come to a stop, and there was Alicia's voice saying "Oh, my God!" in a half cry. Then they were helping me down, and I must have been mumbling something as someone kept me from falling while I stumbled into the house.

"I'll tell you what, Alicia," I heard Jim say from one side. "The next one says he ain't a man I'll kill—if he don't do it first."

Then I was lying down and they were tearing at my clothes, and for one instant I could see her, see Alicia, real clear. I grabbed hold of her wrist and tried to sit up but couldn't.

"I'm . . ."

She put a soft finger across my lips and smiled, a tear rolling down her cheek as she said, "Yes, I know. You're Callahan."

Then everything sort of went black.

7

THE horse just kept galloping away. And there I was alone. Just me and those Colts and my bowie knife. *And the Paiutes.* They were counting coup, coming at me in two single-file columns. There must have been a hundred of them, and I was scared as hell. I shot an even dozen of them, and then I knew I was going to die. As I reached across to pull out my bowie, I yelled, "I'm Callahan!"

I woke up in a cold sweat. I was lying flat on my back, my right hand reaching across the left side of my body to where I kept the bowie knife I carried, like all us Callahans. My hand was squeezed tight around something, but it wasn't my knife. Slowly, I focused my eyes on what it had grabbed hold of, then followed the wrist up the arm and let go. It was Jim.

"That must've been some fight," he said, making light of things the way he did. He was still smiling.

"That's right. Even the wranglers know how you feel about the Paiutes." Alicia spoke from the far side of the room, where she was doing something with some clothes. "And if Mr. Majors had been here to listen to your ravings, I doubt that you'd be working for him much longer."

I remembered what had happened now and where I was. It had been a nightmare, but it was all so real.

"Did I do a lot of . . ." My voice trailed off, for I wasn't all that well yet and didn't think I could speak loudly enough to be heard.

"To put it mildly, *Callahan*, as you insist on being called," Alicia said with a smile, "I heard Jim's account of what he saw of the fight and could only imagine what it must have been like for you. But for the last week I've heard you tell it in graphic description . . . and language." I felt the softness of her hand as she took hold of mine and smiled at me with what must have been relief. "I'm so glad you're better, Sean."

Then I remembered the horse I'd been riding and how it disappeared into that band of warriors after I'd been shot out of the saddle. The mail! I had been so caught up in my own thoughts that I'd completely forgotten about the mail!

"What about the—" I grabbed hold of Jim's wrist again as if holding on for dear life.

"That pony was as tough as you are, hoss. He rode right through those Paiutes and made it here to the station. Hell, he was standing out front when I brought you in." I breathed a sigh of relief, knowing that I hadn't lost the mail on my route.

"Did the next rider make it through?" I felt my voice getting stronger, or maybe it was the urgency I was feeling about getting the mail west. That word "responsibility" had lain heavily on my mind ever since Jim had spoken of it and I had started to ride the Pony.

"No. Matter of fact, the young man who was scheduled to take your route from here on decided he'd had enough of Paiutes for a while and passed on the chance. Can't say as I blame him, either."

After what I'd been through, neither could I. But it was a part of the contract each of us had signed with Russell, Majors, and Waddell. No rider had to take the mail through if there was inclement weather or there was reason to suspect hostiles of one sort or another out there on his route. And it wouldn't reflect on his person at all. It wasn't a matter of bravery or heroism or anything like that; it was simply common sense and a desire to stay alive. And you couldn't blame anyone, whether they were fourteen or forty, for that feeling. Still, there was the question of what happened to the mail if the rider refused his route. I glanced at Jim and then Alicia, who was now bringing a mug of something that looked hot to me. They both knew my next question, and it was Alicia who answered it.

"Jim took the mail through to the next relay." She said it with a pride in her voice that told me she could feel as she did about no one but Jim. Besides, if you couldn't hear it in her voice, you could see it in her face, in the way she looked at him while she spoke. It was about then, foggy-headed and all, that I decided she had one of the prettiest smiles I had ever seen. Jim shrugged it off, and I could tell he wasn't used to receiving this kind of flattery.

"How much time did I lose?" I asked.

Alicia propped me up some and placed the mug in my good hand. It was soup of a sort, although it wasn't familiar to me. But then, my belly had just taken notice that I was alive and, not having eaten for a full week, didn't complain about the makeup of the food one bit.

"About an hour." Jim smiled in that mischievous way he had. "The fella at the relay was madder than a wet hen when I came riding in, wanting to know who the hell I was and why wasn't the mail on time."

"What did you tell him?"

"I told him I lost half an hour's time 'cause it was me riding the pony and the other half was your fault." Here his grin widened. "Told him you spent that time killing off half the Paiute nation. He didn't seem to mind much then. Of course, by the time I was finished, I had my Dragoon in hand and pretty much convinced him that if he made one more complaint it'd be his last."

Alicia smiled at both of us.

"That part I believe," she said, "for Jim can be *quite* persuasive."

There was something in her words that I didn't catch hold of just then, but it was enough to make both of them blush some. I never will know if it was a renewed interest they had taken in each other about then that made them leave or if they just figured I was in need of more rest, but they left me. And I did need the rest.

It was three days before I ventured a try at

getting out of bed. Alicia had thrust a copy of *A Tale of Two Cities*, a new book by Charles Dickens, into my hands and recommended I read it. I did, but in the background I was more than aware of the comings and goings of the riders. It was strangely silent that third day. Oh, there were horses moving about outside, but it wasn't the same kind of movement you hear when a mount is being readied for another rider. And I'll tell you, hoss, some of those mounts were as anxious about the route they'd be traveling as the riders who'd be on them.

Jim had been gone the whole time. But at the end of that third day, just before Alicia was setting the table for her pa and the two wranglers and me, he came riding in. My red shirt and blue pants, the uniform of the Pony rider, were totally worthless now, so I had on an oversized shirt and pair of pants and was trying to see if I could balance myself and practice walking about the room when Jim arrived. I was thinking of how glad I was at least to still have my hat and boots and pistols, when he came in.

"Not bad," he said, taking in my slow, deliberate movements. My left leg was stiff, but I was getting around on it better than I thought

I would. "I suppose next you'll be wanting to ride your route again."

"Why not," I said, almost defiantly. "Won't be a day or two more and I'll be able to get in the saddle and—"

"And you'll still be hobbling around like you are now." His tone was serious. "Don't make light of it, Sean. Both of your brothers have been leg shot and kept on a-going just like you did back there with the Paiutes," he said, throwing a thumb over his shoulder. "But you heed what I'm saying. When it was all over, they had a week or two worth of time to heal up, and if you're wise you'll take the same." What he said made sense, but it didn't do anything for the damnable sense of failure I was feeling again. Hell, I was supposed to be doing a job, and I wasn't, and . . . "I wouldn't worry about it none, though," Jim went on. Like I said, at times Jim could be a real puzzling man, for now he was smiling that impish way he could, the way he did when he knew something that you didn't and he knew that you knew he knew it. It was unsettling.

"It seems that this Paiute war is one that Mr. Majors don't take to kindly," he said. "Fact is, he flat out told the military that if they couldn't furnish some kind of protection for his riders, why, he'd stop service. Don't take to his boys being warred on, I reckon."

"And?" He had me excited now, and I could sense that there was big news coming.

"Well, Sean, it seems those military fellas figured old Majors was bluffing, but he wasn't. As of today, we don't deliver the mail unless there's something done about those Paiutes."

I looked at the calendar on the wall. Alicia had kept it up by crossing off each day, and that made today May 31, 1860. I had mixed feelings at the news, glad on the one hand that the Pony had stopped, for it would give me the necessary time to recover properly. But on the other hand, what if that had been my last ride for the Pony? What if there would be no more rides? I had been riding for this outfit only two months, but it had seemed a lifetime, and I wanted to continue with it. I liked this life, even with the danger and all; I honest to God liked it. Maybe that didn't make much sense, but that's the way I felt, and I never could account for how feelings run. Never could.

"This debate's been going on ever since those hostiles opened up on our riders," Jim continued, "and it looks like we got us some support from the people we're delivering mail for." He pulled out the newspaper he had stuck under his arm all this time, unfolding it and opening it to the page he was interested in. "Here, take a gander at that." He shoved the paper at me, pointing out the article he was interested in. I read aloud:

"The Pony Express is already assuming great importance in California, and large amounts of original drafts are now forwarded by this conveyance. As the usefulness of this quick communication becomes more and more apparent, these valuable trusts will increase.

It is a matter, therefore, of the highest importance that the bold and daring spirits who risk their necks in carrying a sack of letters through the defiles of the mountains, over broken prairies and the rapid rivers which divide us from the Pacific, should be protected. If these gallant fellows cannot perform their circuit unmolested, the Express will have to be abandoned, and the whole country affected thereby. It is bad enough that our government compels the public to rely on private enterprise for this service, when a liberal encouragement in the form of a mail contract should be extended. But to refuse protection afforded by the presence of troops already near the ground would be infamous."

I wasn't quite sure what all those fancy words meant, but I knew that whoever it was that wrote this was on our side. The paper was the Saint Louis *Globe-Democrat*, and Saint Louis was a big town, so I reckoned they knew what they were talking about. Yet in a sense it made me feel strange, for I had never been described as a "daring spirit" and doubted that I ever would be again.

My train of thought was interrupted by a voice in the doorway.

"I told him you was too tough to die." It had a familiar ring to it, and when I looked up, there was Wash Bernard. I started to make my way to the door, saw him raise a hand to slap me on the back and then lower it. "Reckon I better not." We shook hands, and Wash was soon talking a mile a minute, telling me about what he had been doing since I last saw him.

The only distraction we had was from the two wranglers as they came in for supper. They were two older men who kept mostly to themselves. The one with the southern accent brushed past me, bumping into my arm, almost as if on purpose. He stopped briefly, gave a snide look, glanced at his friend, and scoffed. "Chillern," before seating himself at the community table.

We ate supper in silence.

Afterward we broke up into small groups, the wranglers making their way off to one side like they always did, me and Wash setting off to one end of the porch, and Jim and Alicia's pa off on the other end. Alicia was making the rounds with the last of the coffee, filling our cups with it.

Wash had pretty much talked himself out after a while, and as much as I wanted to listen to him, I had other things on my mind. But I reckon when you get to staring out in the distance, well, it ain't too awful hard to tell someone's preoccupied.

"What ya thinking on, Sean?"

"Nothing," I said, still staring off into the setting sun.

Wash nudged me with his elbow.

"Come on, Sean," he urged, "we're friends,

remember? You can tell me." After I said nothing, he went on. "It's those Injuns you shot, ain't it?"

"Yeah. I reckon it is." After all, he was my friend, and as private a matter as it seemed, a body ought to at least be able to tell his friend.

"Oh, don't pay no never mind to them," Wash said. "Fella at one of the stations said they ain't nothing but heathens no way, so it's like they don't count. Here, let me take that." He grabbed the empty coffee cup from my hand and was gone.

Did you ever have a full stomach but feel empty inside? It's a strange feeling, a haunting one, if you know what I mean. Alicia set a fine table, and there was never any lack of food while she was cooking. But that night I was feeling sort of empty. It was after that wrangler had bumped into me and mumbled "Chillern" that I realized that like it or not, I wasn't in that category anymore. I had killed more than one Indian out there on the prairie, and now I was feeling some guilt about it, and it wasn't pleasant. What if they had family like I did? What if I'd taken a son from his father or a father from his son? It wasn't right, and it wasn't a responsibility I would find it easy to live with.

"Right pretty night out," Jim said, easing down beside me. I looked up at the clear, starlit sky, not a cloud in sight. "Near as pretty as Alicia, I reckon." When I didn't comment, he continued. "You know, if someone was to threaten someone as pretty as Alicia, and feeling the way I do about her, why, Sean, I do believe I'd do 'em in. Yes, I would." He said it matter-of-factly, still eying those stars.

"Did Wash—"

"Yeah, he mentioned something to me. But he has good intentions."

For a second the thought passed through my mind that I couldn't trust Wash Bernard anymore at all, but just as quickly I realized that what he had done was out of caring for me as a friend, and that was why Jim was sitting next to me instead of him.

"It sure does get confusing, this growing up stuff."

"Yes, that it does," he said.

I was still looking out into that mass of stars coming out as the last of the sun's light faded into oblivion, yet I could tell that Jim was drawing back on his memory, going over some of his own thoughts.

"I don't know if Nathan ever told you, but I killed my first man saving your life. I was all of nine years old then, pushing ten." That was a story I hadn't heard in the Callahan household, and it surely had my attention now. "We was on the El Brazito down in Mexico, and I was watching the wagon your ma was in, when these Mexican soldiers broke through the ranks and came at us something fierce." His brow knotted up into what could have been a war map, and somehow I had the feeling this wasn't one of his favorite stories. "You was about two minutes into childbirth, and one of those Mexes came up into the wagon and I shot him with Pa's old Paterson. Near got myself killed after that, but Pa and Finn and the others saved us." He paused for a moment, seeing the whole thing over again, and by the look of him I knew it cut hard and fast to the bone.

"It hurt, Sean. Tore me up near as much as that bullet did the fella I killed. Only thing saved me, I reckon, was Grandma telling me that by killing that Mex I'd saved her *and* you." He turned to face me now, his words hard and sure as he spoke. "I ain't going to tell you that

Injuns and Mexes are nothing but lowlifes, 'cause taking a life is taking a life, no matter whose. But I reckon that's part of growing up. You make your decisions when you have to and learn to live with them, right or wrong. It's part of being a man.

"As for the killing, well, I always figured that when your time comes to do it, there ain't much you can do about that. That fella I killed way back then . . . and them Paiutes out there, well their time was up and yours wasn't. The important thing, Sean, is to remember what Finn was telling me about them historians."

"What's that?"

"He says they claim history repeats itself 'cause people keep on making the same mistakes. Way I see it, a body ought to take one look at his history and make sure he learns from what he's done. Come to think of it, you've got to do that out here in order to survive, and you know good and well this is a land of survivors." He stood up and pushed his hat a bit farther back on his head. "So don't dwell on it, Sean. I reckon all of us'll see a lot more death than we ever figured before this land is settled. Besides, there's a lot better things to do with your evenings." I looked up at him, confused now by the smile that crossed his face.

"Huh?"

"Sure. Like hitching your dream to one of them stars."

Then he was gone. What he had said settled in my mind, and I found myself enjoying the evening and its cool breeze.

Or maybe it was those stars I was gazing at.

8

THE one with the southern accent was called the Cajun. Nothing more, just the Cajun. He was close-mouthed except when he got around Wash and me and called us "chillern" like he had that one night. Jim had said there were men like that out here, men who had come from someplace they'd rather not talk about, but that didn't necessarily mean they were hiding something. Some folks were just naturally shy. But I spent a day or two studying these two wranglers while I was trying to get around without looking too much like a cripple, and whether or not they had anything to hide, they were troublemakers as far as I was concerned.

The Cajun's partner was named Reitz. He was tall and nearly as stringy as me at first sight, whereas the Cajun was nearer my size but thick all over. If they were horse handlers, they weren't too good at it, for it seemed as though there was constant turmoil in the corral. With the Pony Express temporarily suspended, Jim had taken advantage of the spare time to bring in more horses, not that it made the work any easier for these two men, and they didn't like it at all. In fact, I didn't doubt that they did some mistreating of horses when me or Wash wasn't around, because some of those mounts got right skittish when they seen the Cajun and Reitz a-heading their way—real skittish.

That the wranglers disliked Jim and barely tolerated Mr. Stiles was evident by the way they snubbed them. I never thought two men who acted and dressed so gruff could act like city snobs, but, hoss, they had the market cornered on it at the home station. That they did. And it didn't take a whole lot of educated guessing to see that sooner or later there'd be trouble.

And there was.

"That must be the widest grin I've seen on you in some time, Sean," Wash said, taking a seat next to me on the steps in front of the house. "But I sure can't see how watching that Cajun would have anything to do with it."

The Cajun was across the yard unsuccessfully trying to work another of the horses Jim had brought in early that morning.

"It's not what he's doing," I said, still

smiling, "it's him, Wash. Believe it or not, it's *him*."

"Now, what in thunder are you talking about, boy?" One thing I'd noticed about Wash since he'd joined us at the station house was that those two months of being on his own had done him good. This wasn't the first time I'd heard it; he was picking up phrases many a seasoned frontiersman used, and enjoying it to boot.

"Well, it's my brother, Finn." I said. "He's the one I told you was the reader of the family." Wash nodded. "He reads all these books about near everything, I reckon."

"What's that got to do with the Cajun?"

"Well, he read a book one time, something to do with science and all, and it said there might be a missing link to the human race."

"And?"

I smiled, looked at the Cajun, and then peered back at Wash. "You ever study him, Wash?"

"No, why?" I had him purely puzzled now.

"Well, I have, and I think he's that missing link."

"Huh?" Now he was even more confused.

My grin widened. "Wash, he ain't got no *neck!*"

At first I thought Wash was going to bust a vein in his own neck, the way he gandered at that wrangler. And when he was through, you'd have thought his eyes were going to fall out! For I wasn't too far from wrong. Like I said, the Cajun was built compactly, and if he had a neck at all, it was only a short inch or two from the base of his skull to his collarbone!

I sat there chuckling to myself until Wash finally got the joke and set to laughing. But that didn't last too long, for it drew a long, hard look from the Cajun. Obviously, he thought we were funning him, and we were, no doubt about it. But from the scowl on his face, I was betting he wasn't one to laugh, not at all.

Maybe my joke was what started it. Or maybe it was just the noon heat that could be devilish hot when it wanted to. There are times it can get to you, and maybe this was one of them.

All I know is that it happened, as I knew it would right from that first mean look the Cajun gave us.

He let go the rope of the horse he was supposed to be working and made a beeline right for me and Wash. I don't know if Wash gave a glance to me, but I didn't even blink an eye at him. I was only watching the Cajun, and at the same time trying to think of what I'd gotten myself into this time.

"You chillern ain't careful," he said, stopping dead in front of us, shaking a hunting knife at us as he spoke, "I'll break you same's we do them hosses down Louisiana." He didn't pronounce it like a Yank would, instead saying something that sounded like "Loose Anna."

"Mister, don't point that thing at me." I said it civilly, but he knew I wasn't funning when I said it. For suddenly I had had about enough of this blowhard, and job or no job, being referred to as a child was sticking in my craw faster than thick-set grits. I was even more surprised when Wash joined in.

"That's right, mister. Mamma said 'twasn't polite."

I had a feeling then that Wash might make a good politician some day, something like Crockett, for he sure was playing the part of a country boy to the hilt. The way he spoke was so innocent and stupid that you'd think a half-brained child had done it, but that wasn't Wash. Not at all.

"We still have work to do, mister," Stiles said from behind us. "You want to chew the fat, do it on your own time."

I hadn't heard Mr. Stiles get angry before, but there was no question that he wanted the Cajun away from us. Perhaps he had been inside watching us and knew what was going on. Whatever the circumstance, the Cajun sheathed his knife and headed back to the horse he was working.

But working horses wasn't what the Cajun had in mind, for there had been that one instant after Stiles spoke when a glimmer passed through his eye, the kind that said he thought he could take on Aaron Stiles and be done with him. Mind you now, Mr. Stiles wasn't much more than medium built, but he did the smithing for the outfit too, and I don't believe I've ever seen forearms as big as his.

Mr. Stiles didn't say much to Wash or me, either, instead disappearing off to someplace or other.

Wash started talking then about how he liked his horses a bit on the wild side when he rode them, for they showed heart that way, and right along with speed, a rider's horse has to have spirit. I nodded yes to what he was saying just to be agreeable with him, but what I was really noticing then was the moves of the Cajun and his friend, Reitz, in the corrals. Then something queer struck me about the whole operation, and I found myself remembering what it was the Cajun had just said.

"Wash?"

"Yeah."

"Ain't those the horses Jim brought in earlier?"

"Yeah, I reckon. Why?"

The mounts that had been frisky that morning now acted quite content, although they still skittered away from the two wranglers. A whole lot of things were running through my mind right then, and I thought I knew what was happening, though it wasn't a pretty thought.

"Ain't these fellas supposed to be breaking those horses?" I asked.

"Yeah, I reckon."

I looked at Wash. "You seen 'em *ride* any of them this morning?"

"No," he said, getting thoughtful all of a sudden. "Come to think of it, I didn't. You don't—"

"Go find Mr. Stiles, Wash," I said, letting myself down onto the ground as easy as I could and grabbing hold of an old cane Alicia had found for me. "Have him come over to the corrals."

Wash saw what was happening then, too, and didn't waste any time palavering about it. Me, I'd decided that there was no way in hell I could take either one of these yahoos, so palavering was what I was going to do until Wash and Mr. Stiles got to the corrals.

"Mister," I said, about halfway across the yard. I would have said it before, but the Cajun hadn't pulled out that hunting knife of his until then. And that knife was what the trouble was if I didn't miss my guess. He looked up at me, frowned suspiciously at the limp in my walk, and put the knife away again.

"Whatcher want, *child*?" he said when I reached the gate. He said it as if I were some nuisance that had gotten in his way. He meant to put a burr under my saddle and had succeeded at it. It dug in hard, and he knew it by the flush that came to my face, but I gritted my teeth, trying to keep from losing my temper.

"How *do* you break your horses in Loose Anna?" Two could play at this game, and by my count I wasn't doing all that bad from the slow red that crept up his neck into his cheeks. I should have waited then, waited for Mr. Stiles like I was going to do in the first place. But I smiled just as recklessly as I'd seen Jim do, and that got him mad.

Two other things happened then, just before the Cajun made his move. Reitz, who'd been having a bad time with a horse at the far end of the corral, took to cussing the animal and flailing it with a whip that all of a sudden appeared in his hand.

And Jim came strolling out of the barn.

"Say, Aaron, I've got the fire going now if you're ready to shoe some of these—" He was as carefree as you please until he saw me standing in front of the Cajun and heard Reitz cussing and using the whip. Turning his attention to the closest wrangler, he spoke to Reitz. "Mister, you put that whip down right now or you're gonna wind up on report to Alex Majors himself." There was no foolishness about him now. Neither of us had grown up liking to see beatings of any kind, and that went for man or animal. Jim was all business now as he headed for Reitz.

The horse he was working with must have known what was in store now, and he reared up as Reitz ignored Jim and went on swinging his whip. I reckon it was a good thing, too, for it caught everyone's attention for a moment and gave me the edge I would need in confronting the Cajun. Jim was up and over that corral fence in no time, grabbing the quirt out of the wrangler's hand as he came down on top of him. But that Jim, he was a quick one, and landed on his feet while Reitz went sprawling. As he fell, Jim did something I'd never seen him do before. There was mad all over his face by now, and I was glad I wasn't Reitz lying there because I'd have caught the leather ends of that whip across my face and felt blood just like the wrangler had coming out of his left cheek now.

"How does it feel, Reitz?" Jim said. I don't know if he was expecting an answer or not, but I don't think he really cared, to tell you the truth, hoss. The wrangler was getting to his feet now as Jim said, "Well, you're going to feel a lot worse before I'm through with you."

I reckon I was paying too much attention to Jim, for that's when I felt a swish of air at my left arm and a light sting as the Cajun said, "That's how we break our horses, *child*," and I saw his knife fly over the fence at me. I knew he'd cut me, and I jumped back out of instinct. Out of the corner of my eye I saw a horse rear up, its front hoof throwing blood into the air, and I knew for sure in that instant that bleeding the mounts was how the Cajun broke their spirit.

It must have been my arm he sliced, but I had no time to notice, for the meanness on his face told me I had my hands full now as he made his way over the corral fence, jumping off the top rail to land full force in front of me.

I don't mind telling you I was scared. I had to have the cane to keep my balance or I would have kicked him. And the wetness I was feeling on my left arm wasn't making reaching for my Navy any easier. He took a wide swipe at me again, and once more I jumped to the rear, nearly losing my balance this time. Somehow it was almost like fighting those Paiutes all over again. Here I was about to die, scared to hell and gone and not sure what I could do about it, and all I could hear was Nathan's words again. Then, for the goddamndest reason, I smiled at him!

"Mister, you're going to know who I am."

That threw him for a second, and that was all I needed. The pain of standing on my left leg was killing me, but I knew what I was going to do—hell, *had* to do—and it didn't matter anymore. I stepped back just a bit with my right foot, flipping that cane end over end in my hand. When I had a firm grip on it, I put all my weight on my left leg and stepped forward, right into the Cajun's swinging area. And when I did, I swung that cane down hard, glad it was made of oak as it landed full force along the side of the Cajun's kneecap. His knee collapsed, and so did the Cajun, but I wasn't through with him yet. He stumbled backward, and when he did, I poked the curved end of that cane handle right into his elsewheres. I didn't have to look at his face to know that the pain was excruciating. It didn't do anything for his disposition either, for he pulled another knife out of nowhere and brought his arm back in an arc that said he was going to plant that knife as deep in me as he could!

A hell of a lot happened in the space of about ten seconds just then. And the loudest thing I heard was the cocking of three guns one after another.

Wash kicked the knife out of the Cajun's hand and stepped up right next to him, cocking his pistol and pointing it at arm's length at the man's heart.

"I could kill you right now, *child*, and it wouldn't even count," Wash said in a serious tone.

The Cajun didn't move, but it wasn't him I was paying attention to. Wash had no sooner spoken up than I heard the second pistol cocked. But this one was from a distance, and when I looked up, it was Reitz pointing his Dragoon at me. With a glance I saw that his face was bloodied all over. Jim had kept his word but looked to be sprawled out himself at the moment. So there I was again ready to die and not knowing what to do. But I didn't have to, for as soon as I heard and saw Reitz with his pistol aimed at me, the third and last gun was cocked. By the time I looked to the porch of the station house, I knew it was a Hawken and that Aaron Stiles was drawing a bead on Reitz.

"You'll never know if you hit him," was all Stiles said. That didn't give the wrangler much time to think, and he didn't use it well, for in that wasted second Jim was up and had his own Dragoon stuck at the man's head.

"And I'll make *sure* of it." His voice wasn't

loud, for that wasn't Jim's way, but there was death, certain death, in the words he spoke. And there wasn't a one of us standing there that would deny it.

Now, some might call that a Mexican standoff, but from where the Cajun and Reitz were positioned just then, I'd be more apt to call it a losing hand, as Jim would say. The Cajun was sweating, still looking down the business end of Wash's Navy, and I couldn't see if Reitz was or not for all the blood on his face, but if he wasn't he should have been. Aaron Stiles made his way across the yard as Reitz lowered his gun. Halfway there he stopped and gave Wash a hard look of his own.

"Put it away, son. If there's any killing to do here, I'll be the one doing it." It wasn't a request as much as a statement of fact.

When he reached Reitz, he took the wrangler's gun and emptied it of its caps before shoving it back into his holster. Jim had put away his gun, and the three were soon standing next to Wash and me as the Cajun lamely got up off the ground.

"I'm not a hard man to get along with," Mr. Stiles said, "but I'll not tolerate men like you who call yourselves workers and ain't. You've both got five minutes to get your gear and get out of my sight. And gentlemen, *I don't ever want to see you again.*"

If there was ever any doubt about who ran that station house, it was gone with Aaron Stiles's handling of the Cajun and Reitz.

In all the excitement I'd forgotten about my arm, but it didn't turn out to be as bad a cut as I'd thought. Alicia had come out by then and was trying to do her best to help me get back into the house, against my protests that I could do for myself. Mr. Stiles and Jim had headed for the barn to shoe some horses, and Wash was feeling proud as could be about saving my life, when the Cajun and Reitz stopped before us on their way out. The Cajun still looked mean as hell, and you couldn't tell how Reitz looked except to say awful hurt.

"You ain't seen the last of us yet, *child*," the Cajun snarled. "Not by a ways."

There was a look of terror in Alicia's eyes as they rode off, and I could understand it well.

For something told me they were right. This wasn't over yet.

9

THE next day I still had a bit of a limp and discovered that getting into fights with men who were bigger than me didn't help the healing process at all. So I took to doing some outriding while Jim and Alicia's pa looked after the station, figuring that I could supply meat for the fire and maybe make up for what I wasn't up to doing.

Where we were was still the Kansas Territory back then, but to hear Nathan talk it was growing fast, what with the gold strike a year and some back, fast enough so it wouldn't be too awful long before folks out here would be wanting their own territory.

And there was still game aplenty, elk and some deer in the high country and buffalo on the plains. Not that I hadn't had my fill of the plains in those two months of riding, but the truth was that I didn't think my body was ready for the traversing of high country just yet, leastwise not on a horse. I was beginning to understand how my brother must have felt when he got shot in the hip and thigh. And I'll tell you, hoss, it don't make you want to go out and march in the first fancy parade you see heading your way! So I stuck to the plains, just a mile or two out from the beginnings of the high country, figuring I might spot some buffalo that had strayed from the herd.

I knew that if I was going to be able to down a buffalo, I'd not do it with one of my Navy Colts. Oh, I still carried them with me, you understand, for I was getting to feel what Jim called "downright naked" without them. I reckon after you've been in a brush with death a time or two, it becomes second nature to reach for your pistol when you find there's a new day ahead of you. My hat, moccasins, and guns were the first things I looked for when I woke up, and I can't say that it was a habit I didn't like. But like Nathan would say, that's a whole 'nother canyon, and it was buffalo hunting I was thinking about then. What I wound up doing, you see, was borrowing Stiles's Colt revolving shotgun. But before I did that I molded some slugs for it that must have run to .58 caliber or more, maybe even in the sixties! One thing I knew for sure when I finished them, and that was that those slugs would tear apart man or beast when they hit . . . and likely leave him wondering what avalanche had hit him while he bled to death, if I didn't kill him outright.

I reckon having a big gun was what gave some men the courage they needed to survive out here, and I'll admit that riding the plains —even by my lonesome—with five of those shotgun slugs by my side gave me a certain feeling of power as I searched for game. But there was something else gnawing at the pit of my stomach and tingling up the back of my spine that morning I went out, and it had nothing to do with my long gun.

You've had the feeling before. I reckon everyone has at one time or another. You're out there minding your own business, when the hairs on the back of your neck stand out like they were bristles on your ma's scrub brush and you get a bit of a chill running up and down your spine. Not a whole lot, you understand, just a bit, for that's the scary part. It's scary because you get this certain feeling that someone *else* is out there watching you. And that in itself isn't all that scary. It's knowing that whoever it is is likely in back of you, and you ain't got the slightest notion whether they're friendly . . . or they're looking to back-shoot you! Well, friend, I had that feeling that first day out on the plains when I set out to put meat on the table. And I'll tell you, it didn't make me sit in the saddle any easier, that's for damn sure.

I tried ignoring the feeling most of the morning and forgot all about it when I came on what looked like a downed buffalo. Turned out he was dead. But that pack of wolves was surely enjoying him. Yessiree, that they were. Now, I never cared for anyone, man or beast, who fed off another of his kind, like buzzards do. And wolves. So I let my mount walk in close enough so them wolves could see me, but it didn't scare them any. Not one bit. A couple of them laid bare their teeth and let out a growl that let me know they'd been there first and I'd better stay away.

It struck me then what my brothers had told me they hated most in men and animals. Arrogance, that was the word Finn used, but he was always good with words anyhow. Nathan, well, I reckon he was like some of us that never had the chance to study every word Noah Webster set down in that dictionary of his, so he made up his own as he went along. And, come to think of it, out here that was as good as anything. Nathan said he couldn't tolerate man nor beast that was "piss ugly mean." And you can bet that caught the women's ears, too. In fact, as I recall, when Nathan said that, both Ma and Ellie turned a quick shade of red and left the room. Me, I knew it was right, and sitting in that saddle watching them wolves snarl like they were doing made me that much surer of what my brother had said. I was in pistol range now, and that's when I pulled out that Navy and shot the eyes out of two of them. That took the bite out of the rest, and they took to the hills like there was no tomorrow.

As much gnawing as they'd done on the buffalo, it was hard telling just how he died or from what. And if he wasn't diseased, those wolves would be back as soon as I left.

It was about then I got that feeling again that I was being watched. But it didn't bring the fear I'd felt before, not this time. There were at least five white men and a whole nation of Paiutes that I'd made enemies of in the past few months, and if any of them had the notion to backshoot me, they'd had more than enough time while I'd done in those wolves. No, whoever it was out there that was eying me, well, they seemed more curious than anything else, I was thinking. Nor did I think they meant any harm.

"I'm leaving now," I said, loud enough for them to hear, and turned to go. There was no reply as my mount and I headed back to the station house, but perhaps that didn't matter. As long as they—whoever "they" were—knew that I knew they were out there. Maybe it would unsettle them enough to make them come forward.

I was still determined to get a buffalo, to pull my weight and supply some food since I wasn't yet able to do my chores around the station. But it wouldn't be an already dead animal I picked up for table meat. For all I knew it could have been the wolves who were rabid; perhaps it was the madness that came with rabies that had made the pack act so desperately. But of one thing I was certain as I rode back to the station. Those wolves served no good purpose and needed to be gotten rid of.

And I was the one who was going to do it.

That afternoon I returned to the spot where I had found the buffalo. The hair on my neck had begun to stand on end again as I approached the area, but it was seeing the dead animal that made me know for sure that someone else had been there.

The buffalo was still there, but a large chunk of meat had been cut from him. And it wasn't animal teeth that had taken it out. That is, not unless a wolf learned himself how to set up to a piece of dead meat and cut some off proper with a good sharp knife.

And if that wasn't enough, there were the two wolves I had killed. They still lay beside the buffalo where they had gone down from my shots, but now they were minus their skins. Who had done it? I found myself slowly scanning the tree line in the distance, wondering if whoever it was that was eyeing me knew I was doing the same to him right then. There didn't look to be anyone visible, but he was there, that much I knew.

But who? Some stray kid who was too scared to come forward, afraid I'd do something to him? Could be. Some hermit who only wished to be left alone? Could be. One thing I was certain of was that it wasn't a man who was in need of assistance, for he would have come forward by now. Whoever it was didn't want me to see him, and if that was his way, so be it. I had enough problems of my own to deal with to want to take on someone else's besides.

I had left the Colt shotgun at the station this time, bringing with me instead a small metal container. I dismounted and began to shake a sparing amount of the contents onto the remains of the buffalo. When I had asked Alicia for some poison, she had given me a small portion of the kind they used to kill rats and such rodents around the station house and barn, and it was that poison I was now sprinkling over the dead buffalo.

It seemed sort of odd to be dealing with death as casually as that when the sight of those open plains and the high country to my rear was such a beautiful thing to behold. Still, I reckon death doesn't make no never mind about the time or place it chooses to happen, so I kept on sprinkling until I had the poison placed over the essential areas I knew the pack of wolves would come after the next time they returned. When I was through, I mounted up again.

"I hope you got enough meat to last you a while, friend," I said in the same loud voice as before, "'cause this here's poison I spread out, and lest you're wanting to be as dead as these wolves, I'd make myself scarce from this carcass."

That was enough warning for anybody who was within hearing distance, and I figured this fella was, so I left it at that.

I reckon there's times a body ought to let curiosity be, for all the grief it can cause you. On the other hand, there's times it's worth following a trail just to see how many turns you have to make before you reach its end.

I was up long before daylight, riding out to where I'd left the buffalo the day before. Part of the reason was to see what kind of damage my poison had done to the wolf pack; the other reason, well, that was curiosity.

I had ridden at any easy pace until I was what I figured to be a hundred yards from where I'd first spotted the downed buffalo. I tethered my horse and walked the rest of the distance to a boulder that would afford protection in case my instincts proved wrong and the lead started flying. By then it was that gray part of the morning that comes just before the sun makes itself known to the world. That was when I saw him come out of the wood line and head toward the dead animals.

He was skinny, likely from being underfed for some time, and just a few inches shorter than me. He pulled a hunting knife from the sheath at his side and took to skinning what looked to be a lot more dead wolves lying about that buffalo. For that much I was glad, for my bait had worked. But the gray was fading now as the sun slowly started to rise, and I watched him as he went about his business. Soon I was able to see his features. And that threw me. At first sight I had figured it to be an Indian, for his hair was dark and long and he was wearing buckskins and moccasins, and the knife was to be expected. But when he stood up, I saw that the hair was braided and they weren't breeches. He was wearing a . . .

"Well, I'll be damned," I said, standing up in plain view as I spoke. I reckon we sort of stood there in a minute taking each other in before deciding what to do about the situation.

I was right about the height, but everything else had been wrong. It was a *she*, by God, and she was wearing buckskins on her lower self all right, but they were in the form of a skirt or some such thing, whatever it is women wrap around that part of them. If she was slight of build, it was because, well, she was a *she*.

Besides, I never seen no brave ever come close to being described as puny and pretty at the same time. She had lines on her forehead, the kind that said she had been around a few days. I figured her for about twice my age, and for some strange reason I found myself taking an interest in this Indian lady. But when I looked at her a second time, I knew why.

"Wasn't for that black hair and three or four inches of growth, ma'am, you'd look a lot like my ma," I said. It came out easy, like it had with Wash once I got to know him. Except I had a feeling that I already knew this woman. But I reckon she didn't want no part of me, for when I took a step toward her, sudden fear came into her eyes, and I saw her give my shotgun a quick glance before she bolted toward the forest she'd come from.

"Wait!" I yelled, and ran after her.

I reckon this was one time when it paid to be young. She was fast, but I outran her in a short time. With the long gun in one hand I reached out and grabbed hold of her shoulder with the other, bringing her to a halt.

"Wait," I said. "I'm not going to hurt you." But the fear was still there, still in her eyes, and for a brief moment I wondered if it would ever leave. Then I let go of her shoulder and set down my shotgun, leaning it against a tree. Smiling never seemed to hurt at times like these, so I did that when I said, "See, I ain't going to do nothing to you." If she bolted this time, I'd let her go.

"Please . . . the furs." She said it in what you'd call broken English, I reckon, not quite sure if what she was saying was conveying what she meant. But then, I would have sounded the same trying to speak Paiute.

"Yeah. Sure." I nodded, not sure what she meant, but I needn't have asked for an explanation, for in a blink she was gone, running in the direction she'd come, back out to the dead wolves. I followed, just taking my time.

She was skinning the last wolf that had died, throwing the hides to one side in a pile when she was done. I found a place to set that scattergun so it wouldn't look so dangerous to her. When I gave her a glance again, she was cutting a piece of that buffalo out.

"No! No!" I yelled, waving my hand. I must have had one hell of a terrified look on my face, for that was the only thing that stopped her from cutting any further. I had no idea how I could explain that she was cutting into poisoned meat. We were silent for a minute then, and I looked down at those animals she had just skinned and shook my head, and I think she got the idea.

"You?" As she looked at me, she used her free hand to indicate that she was shaking something over the buffalo, trying to look like I must have the day before when I shook the poison out of that metal container.

"Yup," I said. "Bad medicine." I frowned to try getting across to her the seriousness of it if she were to eat any more of the meat. What I got in response was a frown of her own, one that was asking me why in hell I had done such a crazy thing, anyway. And to tell the truth, I was damned if I knew how to give her a good reason for it. After all, there isn't much you can do in the way of explaining when you've ruined someone else's food supply. There was more silence before she spoke.

"I know . . . some English." It was the same broken way she had spoken the first time, but her words were clear, not slurred as some would speak.

"You're better off than me, ma'am," I said, back to smiling and trying to get on her good side. "I couldn't speak a lick of Paiute if I wanted to."

Then I reckon we both sort of realized the same thing at once; being that she was a Paiute and I was a white man, we were warring against each other. She must have been seeing in my eyes what I was seeing in hers, the fleeting thought that one or both of us might be dying real quick like. But I'd said I had no intention of hurting her, and I meant it. Besides, I reckon you got to start somewhere if you're going to trust someone.

"Where's your camp?"

When all I got was a questioning look, I picked up two sticks and rubbed them together. She understood then and pointed north into the wooded area. Squatting down, she drew an awkward map, giving directions and what I took to be landmarks I could follow to find the camp. I took one hard look at it, and when I looked up again, she was gathering the furs under her arm, readying to leave. I knew less than I should have about sign language but tried to understand what she was saying.

"Be right there," I said with a polite nod. "Gotta get my hoss first."

I picked up my long gun, took a few steps,

and then realized that the worrisome feeling I had had the day before was no longer with me.

And when I looked back, she was gone.

I had figured I'd find whoever it was that had been following me with their eyes that morning. So I had brought along some bacon strips, and a few homemade biscuits that Alicia was so good at making, and a handful of coffee beans. Now we were finishing it up next to the Indian woman's campfire.

It was outside a thicket and just next to what looked to be a small cave of sorts, although I'd not been inside it yet. It was a good campsite for a temporary, but I couldn't see myself wanting to make such grounds a permanent living quarters. But you do with what you have. Like Jim always said, it's the way of the land.

"It warms me," she said with a smile, finishing off the last of the sourdoughs. I'd had one with a thick slice of bacon and had left the rest for her. She looked like she had lost weight in the wrong places, so I figured that sopping up that bacon grease with the biscuits would help her some. Besides, I was a fairly light eater anyway. At least I thought so.

"Yes, ma'am, it does tend to do that," I said, pouring us more coffee.

That must be the quickest I ever made a friend in my life! There she was with a cup of coffee in one hand, a-looking at me like Alicia did at Jim once in a while. Then she smiled, friendly like, as if we were old hands who had been lifelong friends and hadn't seen each other for a long time. And right then I reckon I was seeing Ma in her face more than her, for I didn't mind the smile at all.

"No," she said, still smiling. "Not ma'am." Then she rattled off what I reckon was her name, and I couldn't catch but the last part of it.

"Rosa?"

She rattled it off again, slower this time, and I tried it but still couldn't get it. When a third try produced even fewer results, she gave a patient smile and said, "Yes, Rosa."

I sighed, feeling some relief at not having to get tangle-foot of the tongue trying to say her name again. If she was willing to settle for Rosa, that was fine with me.

"And you?"

"Oh, Callahan. Sean Callahan." She struggled through it as many times as I had with her name, but with more success, settling for what must have been a working version of Sean or John. It surprised me that she knew that much about the name, and I asked her why.

"I live alone." She shrugged. It crossed my mind that she seemed to think that explained everything, but it didn't.

"I was going to ask where your people were."

"You have nothing to fear from them." The way she said it led me to think it had brought back some bitter memories that she'd rather not go over. "They will not have me. I am . . ."

I could see she was searching for the right word, but even I didn't need Noah Webster and his fancy dictionary to know what it was she was looking for.

"An outcast?" I said it softly, letting it roll out easy so she'd think I was fishing for it as much as she was, even if I wasn't.

"Yes," she said, the smile now gone, replaced by a look of shame. "I took a white man for a husband. The tribe does not allow it."

"Where is he?"

"Gone." There was remorse in her voice as she spoke. I'll tell you, hoss, I didn't know a thing about women or their ways, but right then I had the notion that it was breaking her heart when she said, "After a while not even he wanted me."

"Must be hard." I wasn't sure it was the right thing to say, but it was my turn to say something, and I couldn't think of anything smart to say, like Finn, so I said that. Besides, it was the truth.

"Yes, sometimes it is." It seemed that the more English she spoke the better she got at it, sort of like picking up a rusty old firearm once you've let it set a year or so and ain't fired it. You get to cleaning it up and practicing with it, and it'll plum surprise you how good you are with it after a while. I wondered what it was like to live alone like that and not have anyone to talk to except the stars and maybe yourself. It sure must bring out the need in people, I found myself thinking.

"Seems a shame." I said it while taking in the surroundings, winding up looking at her. But her face was kind of screwed up now, and I could tell she didn't understand what I meant. "What I was thinking, Rosa, was . . . well, most everyone I know's got a need for someone. Jim, that's my kin, he's got this girl name of Alicia, see, and he really likes her. And . . . well, I reckon I never seen someone didn't need someone else." It was clumsy the way I said it, but no one could ever say I shied away from the truth, even if it wasn't spoken in proper English.

"You are right," she said, nodding her head slowly. "People *do* need others." She had a sad look about her now, and I thought I saw a tear form in her eye, thought I could feel her heart break as she said, "But sometimes it is not always for the best."

She was silent then, but just before she turned away I saw a tear roll down her cheek and heard what I thought was a sob. Maybe some of the white man's ways had rubbed off on her, for these Indians, especially the women, could be real emotionless, I'd heard.

I never will know why I did it. Maybe because I needed to or because she was needing it and didn't want to admit it or pass off her troubles onto anyone else. But I did it just the same. I stood up and walked around that campfire to her and lifted her chin as gently as I could until I was looking down into her eyes, water still flowing out of them like it was flood season on the Missouri.

"It'll be all right," I said, hoping I wasn't making the fool out of myself that I felt.

Then I got my rifle and left.

But you know something, friend, I do believe that was the first time in my life I'd ever felt something for a woman other than my ma. For I had a strange feeling riding back to the station that day, one that was there but that I couldn't explain.

Like Rosa said, it warmed me.

She wasn't fixed for much more than living one day at a time, so I spent the rest of the week hunting. And visiting. By the third day it seemed like clockwork the way the hours would go. By midmorning I'd come upon a buffalo and let fly one of those shot-shell rounds and killed him. You dare not waste in this land, and I made do with every bit of those beasts I could put that bowie knife to. It took a couple of hours to get the most of what I could use, but I supplied enough meat for both Rosa *and* the Stiles table with what I brought in. The skins I left with Rosa, and after that first day there was coffee boiling when I rode into her camp. It made me feel good when I did, for she had a smile for me. And sometimes, hoss, there ain't nothing that's worth more than that. Especially if it makes you feel like you fill someone else's needs, and that was how I was feeling.

I brought a dictionary out with me, and we spent the afternoons teaching each other. I taught her a few more basic words, and she taught me sign language so I'd be able to get along better on the plains if I should have occasion to talk to some peaceful Indians.

And we talked. About a lot of things. One day my curiosity got the better of me, and I explained how some of those Paiutes had simply ridden after me and others were flat-out warlike and killing mean.

"How come they chase us? The Pony riders?"

"The ones who are warlike want nothing more than to kill you for what was done to their families. It is unfair, but it is war . . . and nothing is fair in war.

"Those who chase you are only curious. They want to know what it is that you carry in the little boxes that makes you ride so fast. I suspect they think it is some kind of power and want it for their own use."

So I explained to her about the letters we carried and how they were not meant to harm anyone. Still, I knew that the Paiutes would likely continue to chase us anyway unless the army sent out patrols to keep them away.

Much as I wanted to be riding again, I didn't want to stop visiting this Indian lady, Paiute or not. But at the end of the week word came in that the Indian raids would be decreasing now that the cavalry had lent a hand to the frontier defense and made its presence known. Jim told me I'd be scheduled for a ride the next day, and I can't say as I was real happy heading out toward Rosa's camp that last time.

I didn't take Noah Webster with me that day, for all I had in mind was leaving Rosa with a good supply of food and saying goodbye. I had enjoyed talking with her and had learned much from her, about the Paiutes, the frontier, and myself. She was an independent woman and much older than I and a free spirit, I reckon you'd say. We'd treated each other as friends for that short time, but now I had to get back to my own mission of riding for the Pony. I didn't know whether I'd ever see her again, but I wanted her to know that I had enjoyed making her feel wanted again, for by then I honestly believed she had that feeling about her.

When I brought the meat in, I set it down

and headed for the small creek nearby to wash myself off. As usual, Rosa had coffee on the fire and a tender smile on her face. But today I only looked away, not wanting her to see my sadness.

"Something is wrong?" She said it from behind me as I shook my arm free of water.

"I'll be riding again tomorrow," I said, looking over my shoulder. "The Pony is going to start sending the mail through again."

At the campfire she had some meat roasted and poured coffee for us. But today she didn't eat; instead, she sat across the flames, studying me, studying my face. Neither of us spoke until I had finished eating.

"Where is your Noah Webster?"

I shrugged. "I just wanted to bring in a supply of meat and say goodbye. There's a lot has to be done yet."

"You do not think you will see me again?" It was a statement of fact or a question, maybe both. I didn't know, I just wanted to get out of there, for I was beginning to feel the way she had that first day I'd met her.

"Who knows. There are a lot of riders getting shifted about, a lot of them quitting because of this Indian war business. Never can tell." I was studying my coffee, although I'll be damned if I knew why, for there sure wasn't any answer in those grounds. I reckon I just didn't want to face up to her, one way or the other. Then she came over and sat down beside me, taking the coffee cup from my hand. Setting it next to the fire, she ran a hand over my chin, smiling at me as she did.

"The first day you held my chin like this and said it would be all right." Slowly she withdrew her hand. "And it was. It is." A serious look came over her now as she looked into my eyes. "But you must never say goodbye unless it is *forever*."

I didn't know what she meant, suddenly feeling like the confused one. How could you tell if goodbye was forever? How could you know one way or another if you'd ever see someone again, unless maybe you were Jim or Alicia? I didn't know what lay in store for me tomorrow. What if I got shot out of the saddle like the last time and never lived to tell of it? Or what if I never saw another Indian again as long as I lived? What if . . .

But there didn't seem to be time for thinking or even finding any answers, for if I didn't understand what was going on, Rosa surely did.

Now she had my hand in hers, rising and pulling me behind her. When she was in front of the cave, she faced me, an almost pleasant look on her face. She was no longer fearful or shameful or shy. She was sure of her independence and knew it; I could tell that much about her. With a warm smile, she took both my hands in hers.

"Some things, Sean, are better left for nature to explain." That was all she said. And she said nothing else until I left.

Now, hoss, I didn't have my Noah Webster with me that afternoon, but I'll tell you one thing. It was a real education.

And the longest goodbye I ever said.

10

I ONCE heard my brother say that any man who became a legend in his own time usually didn't live that long. I never was sure if he was joshing or serious, but after what I'd been hearing about "Captain" Jack Slade, well, hoss, stories like that made me wonder if maybe he was becoming a legend in his own time, anyway.

Like I said, he ran the home station on the west side of my route. I only met him twice more after the Pony started up again, but they were times I'd not soon forget, and they were proof of one thing I was finding out more and more—that some men were respected in this wild land and that they were men who could be hard but fair. And from what I'd heard, that was Jack Slade.

His station was north of Denver, located on the overland stage route. The station house was a fair-size building, as were the barns and corrals that surrounded it, since Slade's stop served the overland stages as well as the Pony

Express. The times I had been there after I'd first met him, he had been off on some errand someplace and I had caught a rider coming in with eastbound mail and had had little time to stick around.

Jack Slade wasn't awfully big, but I reckon legend does that to a person, makes them stomp bigger tracks than they are capable of making with their own body. Still, there was the story about how Slade was out buying hay for the line when he discovered that a bunch of bushes had been covered with hay by the rancher selling it to him, who had figured on making a profit on it. Well, they say Slade got hold of that rancher right quick and tied him up to that false stack of hay and said he was going to burn the man alive after he got through taking what hay he'd paid for originally. And that rancher, he got to whimpering and begging like a child. But Slade said the only way he'd spare the man's life was if he got out of the territory then and there. And that's just what the man did.

The first time I had met him, he hadn't seemed all that big. Fact is, when I got to him this time he looked kind of small and bloodied as hell.

I was just riding into the station, when five

shots came from inside the station house, causing my mount to shy as I pulled up in front. A westbound rider grabbed the mochilas from my horse and threw them on his as he started his route. I was so caught up with the shooting that I didn't even notice who it was that was riding. All I knew was that something wasn't right inside. By the time I was heading for the door, I had my Navy in hand.

A man was backing out the door as I approached. Just past him I saw Slade, lying on the floor all bloodied by what looked to be about five different holes that were pouring liquid red from his body. I didn't see the shotgun until it went off, and then it was too late. The man coming out the door had it in his hands and let fly a load of double-O buckshot that hit Slade full in the chest, making me wonder if he wouldn't lose most of himself to the floorboards.

"When he's dead," the man with the shotgun said, "you can put him in one of those dry-goods boxes and bury him."

Now, friend, I didn't know this fella from Adam, and the way he was grinning, he could have been Satan himself. But one thing I did know was that you don't go putting five slugs and a load of buckshot into a man's front unless you're one hell of a good shot . . . or a bushwhacker. And I'd grown up having no love for bushwhackers, so there wasn't any question about what to do.

I stuck my Navy in the man's back.

"Easy, friend," I said as conversationally as I could manage as his body went stiff. "Now you set that scattergun down real gentle and just stand still."

While he did as I told him, the overland stage pulled up in front of the station house and some men picked up Slade and laid him on a bunk. You couldn't see much of him for the blood, and I'll tell you, hoss, if he wasn't dead, he damn sure ought to have been! That's why what happened next seemed sort of like a miracle, in a way. You see, that was when Slade propped himself up on his elbows, and from the look about him, I reckon he didn't take to the sneer on the bushwhacker's face any more than I did.

"Damn you, Jules," he said in a wheezy gasp that still managed to be hard, "I shall live long enough to wear one of your ears on my watch guard. You needn't trouble yourself about my burial." Then he sank back down on the bunk, and I thought he was dead. I honest to God did!

"What's going on here?" a man behind me asked. He was an older man and must have gotten off the stage, for I'd not seen him at the station before.

"And who might you be?" I said it as friendly as I could, still holding my Navy in this Jules fella's back.

"I'm the superintendent of this stage line." If he was trying to sound impressive, he got his point across. "And you are?"

"Sean Callahan. I ride for the Pony." I figure if you want to impress someone, you hit them between the eyes with a good thick piece of oak wood. Works fine on jackasses, Nathan said. So I just told this fella the truth. "You'll pardon me if I don't offer you my hand, but this fella just did some killing, and I never did get fond of it."

"That so." The superintendent turned the man around by the shoulder so he could see his face and then nodded as if confirming his belief. "Jules Reni. I should have known." With that he pulled out his own gun and gave this Reni character more to worry about. "I'll take care of him now. Mr. Callahan." With that he pulled

Jules Reni away, muttering something to the effect that the man was now under arrest and about to be hanged for murder.

One thing I was finding out was that you could never tell about a man. Some men are set in their ways and just flat too mean to die, sort of like Nathan and this Slade fella, who now had a couple of men pulling lead enough out of him to open their own mine. Then there's some that are all talk. But this superintendent, I had him figured for a doer, otherwise he wouldn't be in the position he was. After I looked in on Slade and was told I couldn't do anything for him, I walked back outside and saw that I was right. The stage line superintendent was a doer.

He and some of the men with him had thrown a rope over a piece of hard wood and were attempting to give this Jules Reni a slow death. Three times they pulled down on that rope, hauling Reni up off the ground until his face turned blue. And three times they let him back down because his neck didn't break! That experience was enough to make Reni give that superintendent his word he was leaving the country, which was the only reason the man let him go.

I do believe that was one of the strangest hangings I've ever seen in my life.

News had it that Jack Slade lingered on for a few weeks hovering between life and death before he was finally sent to some fancy hospital in Saint Louis. He was there a month or more before returning to his home station, and when he did, the whole fight between him and Jules Reni got fired up again. Mostly by Jules Reni, who was boasting that he was going to do in Slade in any fashion he could.

According to Jim, Jules Reni was a pretty popular man around the town of Julesburg, which had been named for him. A French Canadian with a hot temper, he was pretty much taken to be the leader in that part of the territory, taking care of disputes for those who where his friends and doing in those who weren't.

"Reni's been spreading the word that he's collecting cattle," Jim said one day, "but most people know what he's up to."

"What's that?"

"Well, there aren't any brands on them, but it's Slade's cattle he's been rounding up. And he's doing it for one reason and one reason alone."

"To get Slade to come after him."

"That's right, Sean." Jim smiled. "But I think old Jules has got a surprise coming to him."

"How's that?"

"Well, I reckon getting shot does certain things to a man. Some it'll make skittish about getting into a situation where they might have to open the ball again. And I reckon there's some who would go into pure hibernation once they recovered." Here he paused and gave that lazy smile of his.

"Jim," I said, "you've got the damndest way of telling a story."

"I was just thinking," he said, still smiling. "That third breed of men is like Pa and this Slade character. They'll get shot all to hell and gone and pull out the lead themselves if they have to. But when they get through, why, they'll charge the devil himself, grab his pitchfork away from him, and tack him to the wall with it and leave him hanging—by his elsewheres." Even I had to smile at that. "And you mark my words, Slade is as intent on killing Jules Reni as the Reni is eager to do him in."

Jim was right.

I was waiting at Slade's home station one day, when I met him a third time. There was an eastbound rider due in any minute, and when he arrived the relay I was riding would commence. But in the meantime I was standing out front, just leaning up against the wall when two riders came in with a third one between them. The third man was Jules Reni, and he didn't look none too happy about his station in life just then. The riders dismounted, taking the man around back to the corrals. One or two of Slade's hands followed, and for a minute I was tempted to go also, but there had been enough late mail going through of late to make me want to be on time.

A few minutes later the overland stage pulled in, with "Captain" Jack Slade at the reins. Now, Jim told me that he'd met Slade once and that the man had seemed friendly as could be, but I'll tell you, hoss, the look he was carrying now was pure revenge, and I could tell he was going to have some fun at it.

If there was ever someone with a purpose in life, it was the man who got down off that coach, looked briefly around, and seemed to decide just what it was he had to do. Like I said, I was leaning up against the building waiting for that rider to come in. I'll never know why, but Slade walked right past me and yanked one of my Navy Colts out of its holster, saying, "I want this," as he did. As soon as he'd grabbed it, he stopped short to check the loads, giving me the most god-awful stare out of the corner of his eye that I'd ever seen. It was almost as if he were daring me to take my own gun away from him. When he was sure that the gun had enough rounds in it, he walked around the corner of the building, using the same path as the men who had just brought in Jules Reni. That was when I decided that the eastbound rider could wait a minute when he came in. I wasn't going anywhere without that pistol of mine, so I followed Slade around to the back of the corral.

And I'll tell you, friend, this was the damndest shooting you've ever seen!

Those two men holding Reni got out of the way right quick when Slade came into view; come to think of it, Reni didn't look none too pleased, either. That was when Slade took dead aim on Reni in what looked to be a head shot, and fired. Now, you'd have thought that Reni would have been dead when he fell backward, but for some strange reason, the bullet had ricocheted off his tooth—or something in his mouth—and he was still alive!

"I haven't hurt you," Slade said, nearing the fallen man, "and no deception is necessary. I have determined to kill you, but having failed in this shot, I will now, if you wish it, give you time to make your will."

Aside from the two who had brought Reni in and Slade's hands, there was another man, likely a passenger from the stagecoach, standing by. I don't reckon any of us believed what we were seeing, but this city man said he'd go get the fixings for the will and make it out for Reni. When he disappeared, Slade raised and cocked the pistol with all the deliberateness in the world and shot Jules Reni between the eyes.

Jules Reni would not need the paper and pen.

"Injuns got the best belief," Slade said to me, handing the pistol to me butt first. With the same deliberateness that he had said his final words to Reni, he now spoke to me, and I don't mind telling you that it was downright scary indeed.

"What's that Mr. Slade?" I tried to sound as polite as I could, not wanting to get on his bad side.

"Callahan!" a man yelled from the front of the station. "I got your mount ready, and the rider's in!"

"In a minute!" I yelled back at him. Right now my attention was riveted on Slade.

"Never lie and never quit." That was all he said before he walked away.

Never lie and never quit. I thought about that as I reloaded and jumped on that pony to begin my ride. It didn't seem like a bad way of life if you thought about it. Not bad at all.

And those are five words I never forgot.

11

LOOKING back on the three weeks the Pony had temporarily stopped its mail delivery, I'd remember how my vacation time had been filled with excitement. Still, it was good to be riding with those lads my age. And quite a bunch they were.

There was Johnny Fry, who seemed to be quite handsome to the young ladies along the route. At first the girls took to baking for him, but that got to be bothersome after a time. After all, a rider had all of two minutes to down a fast cup of coffee if it was available, not to mention emptying his vitals, before riding on. So you can see how that might have led to problems when a young lady was offering you a whole pie. But that didn't stop those girls at all, nosiree. Why, they took to making sugar cakes and punching a hole out of the center so Johnny could ride along and just grab up a whole stick full of them.

The latest story about Johnny Fry and those romantic young ladies was that one of those girls had taken to making a patchwork quilt and had wanted to sew a piece of Johnny's shirt onto it. He refused, but the girl was determined, and once while he was switching mounts, she ran right out and tore off his shirttail as he mounted up and rode away. Most of us who heard it thought it a good yarn, although I never did hear Johnny's side of the story.

But if Johnny Fry was popular with the girls, it was "Pony" Bob Haslam who had gained a reputation for being a long rider, even during the Indian wars that spring. On one ride he had come across hard times, finding a rider who didn't care to risk his scalp that day because of the Paiute uprising, and found at the next station that the horses had all been commandeered to fight the Indians. But Bob, he kept on going, traveling a full two hundred miles on only two different relays before reaching his destination. Trouble was that after an hour and a half of sleep the station master had him on his feet again and he was riding the same route, only eastbound this time. And he made the same ride back to his original destination.

There was also a young lad by the name of Bill Cody who was in the process of becoming a well-known rider. But it was Wash Bernard I enjoyed being with most. And we'd made a few long runs between us, too.

"Feels good to get some time off now and again, don't it?" Wash said after we'd been back to riding for a few months. Our schedules were such that for a few hours one afternoon at the Stiles station Wash and I didn't have any rides to make, so we spent our time swapping stories we'd heard about other Pony riders.

"What do you mean?" I asked. "Why, you've been off near every third day."

"My eye and Betty Martin! It's you that ain't been riding but two out of three days. I've made every one of my rides," he said defiantly.

"We'll see about that," I said, and hailed Jim, who was crossing the yard.

"What can I do for you, boys?" He had filled the gap since Mr. Stiles had fired the Cajun and Reitz, doing as good a job or better as a wrangler than those two blowhards had ever done. But I had a feeling that Aaron Stiles knew as well as I did that it was really Alicia who Jim was staying on for. Evidence of it was the more than bright mood he had been in since taking the job.

"Has Wash made all of his runs?"

Jim shrugged. "Yeah. Everyone's been on

time. No lag time, no bother from the Paiutes. I'd say we're running in some pretty good luck this month."

"But—" I stopped, an almost impossible thought crossing my mind.

"But what?"

"Nothing, Jim. Nothing." I must have sounded as worried as I was feeling right then, for Jim cocked an eye in my direction.

"You sure?" he asked suspiciously.

"I think I know what he's getting at, Jim," Wash said, "and if I'm thinking the same thing, it's kind of spooky." Jim frowned for a moment, puzzled, but I knew we had his interest.

"It's just that Wash says he's made all of his runs and I've made all of mine," I said, trying not to sound too foolish, "but ain't neither of us seen the other on our night runs. And that's every third night."

Jim nodded the way he did when he had a problem figured out, smiling all the while.

"Better get used to it, lads," he said. "You're riding long hours now, and your body's getting used to what the rest of nature, especially your horses, already knows."

Wash and I exchanged puzzled glances.

"Were I a betting man, I'd lay odds you two have been passing each other in the night sound asleep to the world. You two were just getting some rest while you could. Of course, you've got to have a goodly bit of confidence in your mount to know he's gonna take you through safely. But then, we've got surefooted, commonsense stock here, so don't worry about it none."

Wash and I were looking at each other again, this time in disbelief as Jim went back to work. If what Jim had said was true, and I'd no reason to doubt him, I had just gained a whole new faith in the half-broken, half-wild mustangs we were riding.

But it wouldn't be long before that faith was put to a test . . . and my life on the line.

12

AT one point that summer, June or July, I forget which, word came down that a rider had gone through the Rockies and encountered a first-class snowstorm. It seemed like a relief since the weather was so hot for those of us riding on the plains, but as the summer passed and the furnacelike desert began to cool off with the coming of autumn, I found myself wondering just what that rider had gone through in that summer snowstorm. I had grown up around the area that was now becoming a boom town called Denver and was no stranger to the Rocky Mountains. On more than one occasion I had accompanied Nathan or Finn or Jim—and sometimes all three—on hunting trips into the mountains. Still, those trips hadn't been of the frequency of the likes of Carson, Bridger, or Smith in their days as fur trappers, and I wasn't all that familiar with the territory *north* of Denver in the Rocky range. Yet I knew that when winter set in, I'd be riding through that country, for the central overland route we'd been following was still the quickest way to get east or west for a Pony rider or a stagecoach.

It wasn't the cold I would mind so much as the snow. With as many ravines and dead-end canyons and cliffs you could ride to your death over as I heard there were in that part of the country, it would be hard enough trying to keep a sense of direction during the heat of the summer. It was knowing that when snow covered everything in God's creation it would be twice as hard keeping to the trail that made me start to get as skittish as some of the mustangs I'd ridden.

I was pondering that subject—or trying to stay busy enough *not* to—when I found out how much people can surprise you. It was downright uncanny. Or maybe it just seemed that way because I was still pretty young.

Some people are predictable, set in their ways, I reckon you'd say. Like the Cajun and Reitz. And those two plug-uglies we'd had a run-in with back in Saint Joe, Rodell and Hardin. Just thinking about them brought to mind something I'd heard Finn say. According to my brother, anyone who didn't change his mind about *something* over a ten-year period ought to be pronounced brain dead. And if there was anyone that statement described, it was those four. The only things they knew were their own pure hatred of others and wanting to have their way about anything and everything that pleased them. They had no respect for other folks, and I had a feeling that those they came into contact with had little use for them as well. I know I sure didn't.

Then there are people who surprise you right when you think you've got them figured. One of those people, for me at least, was Rosa. I had genuinely enjoyed her company that week last summer, and I'd learned quite a bit from her. What made me feel even better was knowing that she felt she had learned from me as well. I wasn't sure if that notion was just one a foolish fourteen-year-old would hold on to or if it was a grown-up idea, but I suspected it would make anyone feel proud to have taught someone else something useful.

But when that week was up and I had to leave, I didn't think I'd ever see her again. After all, she was what you'd call unwanted in both worlds, the white man's and the red man's. She was the first of that kind I had run into, and I naturally assumed that she would go on about her business as she had before and that I would be a short-lived memory to her as she continued her life. The fact is that I had only thought of her fleetingly now and then. So it was quite a surprise to see her at the home station when I returned from a ride late that fall. And all of a sudden my memories of the time I had spent with her were as vivid as yesterday.

"What are you doing here?" I asked, seeing her there on the steps to the house. Then, remembering the urgency of this particular ride, I turned to the rider who would carry the mail west from here. "Get it through as fast as you can, Ray. They're saying this is an important run."

"How so?" he asked, jumping into the saddle of a fresh mount.

"It's the election. They say Lincoln won it."

"You bet, pard." He said it with confidence, the kind that many of us were getting a good dose of, and then he was gone.

When I turned back to the house, Rosa was in my arms, hugging me. And I must have turned a dark shade of purple from the neck up, for over her shoulder I could see the smiling faces of Jim, Alicia, and her pa as they gazed down at us. When I finally pushed her away from me, I didn't know what to say or do. It was Rosa who spoke first.

"It is good to see you . . . Sean." She smiled, speaking better English than I ever believed I could teach. At first I thought it was pride about her accomplishment that made me feel kind of warm inside, but looking at her standing full in front of me there, well, I got to wondering if maybe it wasn't something else that had provided that feeling.

"You'd better come in before you catch your death," Alicia said, embracing herself with her arms. I hadn't noticed it until then, but there was a bit more chill to the air than usual. "I've coffee and bear sign on the table for you."

"Bear sign" is what we called those fancy pastries Johnny Fry's girls were making with a hole in the center and calling doughnuts. But when you got right down to it, it didn't matter a lick what you called them, for when a body could scare up a woman's cooking, well, hoss, it was better to eat it while it was hot than to argue about its name! And the more meals I ate of Alicia's, the more I was getting to appreciate her cooking.

The food was good, the coffee was hot, and

Alicia kept my cup filled without even asking. I ate as much as I dared without getting bloated. Meanwhile, Jim took care of my mount, and Aaron Stiles excused himself to do some other chores. That left me and the women the only ones in the room. Wash must have been off on a ride, for he was nowhere in sight.

Rosa wasn't nearly as pretty as Alicia, yet I found myself with that warm feeling in me, which couldn't possibly have been put there by the coffee or food. I sat staring at the bottom of my cup and wondering if this was the way Jim felt about Alicia. If it was, I didn't blame him one bit for smiling every time she came into view. Rosa wasn't even half as pretty, yet I had the same feeling. How could it be? Ellie and Tally, Nathan and Finn's wives, both were as beautiful as could be. Now, I never had asked my brothers just why they fell in love with those particular women, but it only seemed logical to carry the notion that a goodly part of it was due to the beauty of the women themselves. So there I sat, puzzled by the whole situation, not to mention by my own feelings.

"I have a surprise," Rosa said as she rose from across the table.

"Yes, Sean," Alicia said, pouring more coffee

as the Indian woman disappeared from the room momentarily. "Your Rosa is quite a lady." There was a pride in the way she said it, as though she wanted me to know that she was glad she had met both Rosa and me, but the first thing that crossed my mind was that she knew more about us than I might want to let be known. Not that I was ashamed, you understand, it was just that . . . Damn, but life was getting complicated!

"For you," was all Rosa said when she returned, placing an armful of furs on the table and disappearing again.

I immediately recognized the wolfskins as having belonged to the animals I had poisoned that summer, but for the life of me I couldn't see what good they'd do me in that pile. So I started sorting them out, finding that the furs had been cut, fashioned, and designed to be used as leggings, to cover leggings, I reckon. I could see by the smile on Alicia's face that she knew all about it and was quite proud of it. I reckon the look on my face told her I was pretty well impressed with the whole idea, too. Next to seeing Rosa there in the first place, I reckon this was as pleasant a surprise as I'd had in a long time. But it was only the beginning, for when the Indian woman returned this time, it was with an armful of robes that had been fashioned from the buffalo I had killed that summer. A third trip produced two more similar robes. By their looks they were of varying sizes, and that meant there was likely one for each of us in that pile. A look of pride was now on Rosa's face as she glanced at the pile of buffalo skins, up at Alicia and me, and then back at the robes again before speaking.

"For you . . . all," she said with a sweeping gesture of her hand that took in the whole house.

Alicia nearly dropped the coffeepot, so I took it from her and found its rightful place on the stove while she and Rosa hugged each other and shed some tears the way a woman will when she's happy crying. When Alicia was through with her, it was me Rosa was hugging for what seemed an awful long time before she stepped back, smiled, and gave me a short kiss on the cheek.

"Well, now, you're just full of surprises, ain't you," I said, not sure of what else I could say that would make sense. But Rosa just smiled, and I reckon we stood looking at each other in silence until Alicia entered the room with Jim and her pa in tow.

"They didn't believe me," she said as the two stood awestruck at the sight that lay before them. Alicia closed the door, and pretty soon you'd have thought it was a family reunion that was going on. Or maybe Christmas being celebrated a bit early, the way everyone was excited and all, passing the robes around to make sure the right one fit the right person. There was even one left, it being for Wash, I reckon.

The robes fit just snugly enough to keep a body warm and still have room for a Colt at the hip in case the need arose. Rosa had made good use of her Indian ways and common sense, making use of every possible part of the animal that she could. But as the gaiety died down some, I thought I saw a look of sadness come into Rosa's eyes. When I looked across the room at her, frowning at what might be running through her mind, she saw my face and then began walking toward the door. It only took me three strides to reach it the same time she did.

"I must go," she said. There was still a sadness about her, but now I knew what it was. It wasn't for anything she had done but rather for what she thought she could not do. In her mind, in her world, she had done a kindness, but that was all. Now it was done, and it was time to return to where she had come from; if she was sad, it wasn't because she wanted to go but because she had to. In her world that was the way of things.

"No!" There was defiance in Alicia's voice as she spoke up. "No, you must stay." She looked at us as if waiting to hear us speak, but not a one of us did, for we were waiting to hear her out. "Here, with us," she continued. There was another pause and more silence before she turned to Aaron. "Father?" I reckon she figured she'd done as much as she could, and now it was her pa's decision, which was as it should be.

"Well," he stammered, sounding as unsure as I had earlier, "where do you live?" He was addressing Rosa, but she only looked at me.

"She's living in a small cave at the back of one of those wood lines just off the prairie a few miles from here."

"A cave?" he said incredulously. "You brought all these furs here to us and you're freezing in a cave!" It was both a question and an exclamation of wonder. And I reckon it was hearing his own words that made up Aaron Stiles's mind right then and there. "Well, now, ma'am, I reckon we'll fix that up right quick." Rosa gave me a puzzled look as the station manager continued. "Jim, what say you saddle up three mounts and let's go get this lady's valuables."

"Sounds like a good idea," Jim said agreeably, and was soon gone. It was Aaron Stiles who escorted Rosa out to the horses a short time later, and between the two of them, I don't think I could tell who was happier, Rosa or Alicia.

"It'll be so good to have a woman around the house to talk with," Alicia said, closing the door.

"I reckon it does get right lonesome for a woman out here."

"Yes, it does, Sean," she said, clearing away the table. "I don't know what I'd do if it weren't for Jim."

She washed the dishes in silence while I found a towel and gave her a hand drying them. It was getting on toward sundown by then, and I still wasn't all that sure about what had happened that afternoon concerning my feelings. There were still a lot of questions I wanted to ask but dared not for fear of being made a fool of.

"Why the frown, Sean?" she asked as I dried the last plate. "I thought you'd be happy about what Rosa had done for you."

"I am," I said, but then the frown was there again. "It's just that . . . well, this growing up stuff is harder than I figured."

"Oh? And how's that?" There was a smile coming to her face now, and I could feel the back of my neck getting slowly red.

"Like now," I said, and it must have sounded defensive at best. "Whenever I get to asking something, why, it sounds stupid."

"And how do you know that?" It was as if I'd offended her personally.

"By the look on your face. You people get to smiling or looking like you're expecting something foolish to be said, and it's me who's doing the talking, and—"

"Sean." I didn't interrupt other people and didn't expect it to be done to me, but when she put a soft hand on mine and sat down at the table, I shut up and followed suit. By the time she was seated, the grin was gone, replaced by a serious look now. "How old are you?"

"I'll be fourteen next month." So what if I

wasn't quite fourteen? I'd been within reach of it for six months now.

"Well, that makes me all of three years older than you."

I frowned, though she didn't sound smart-alecky when she said it, as some would.

"I don't understand." And I honest to God didn't.

"Don't you worry none about what people think or what they say to or about you. I know what you're feeling, and I sometimes feel that way yet myself." She paused here and squeezed my hand, but somehow I knew that it was a different kind of feeling from what she conveyed to Jim, almost like she wanted us to be friends and wouldn't pass on advice like this to anyone but a good friend. "When the time comes, you'll say and do the right things just because you're you"—-and here she smiled—"and a Callahan. I know Jim's had a good upbringing, and I suspect you have too, so don't you ever be ashamed to speak your mind."

"I think I know what you mean," I said, pushing myself away from the table.

"And Sean?"

I looked down at her, still seated at the table. "Ma'am?"

"You always remember one thing. The only foolish question is the one that's *not* asked."

What she was saying made sense, and I found myself believing that I'd made an honest to goodness friend that night in Alicia Stiles.

"Yes, ma'am." I smiled and was about to leave the room, when a question came to me and I knew that Alicia would know the answer to it. "You mind if I ask you something, Alicia?"

"Why, of course not."

"You like Jim a lot, don't you?"

She blushed now, a smile coming to her face. "Yes, Sean, I like him. In fact, I'd say I love him."

"What makes you say that?"

"Well, because I, I—" She stopped for a minute then, staring off into the distance, and from the look about her I gauged this was the first time she'd asked herself that question, too. But when she spoke next, it was with the confidence of a woman who knows what she is about. "Because I want to *do* for him. Because he is a good and gentle man, and I think, no, I *know* he is good for me. And I can be just as good for him. Because I want to be with him forever. That, Sean, is what makes me say I love him."

I had to digest what she said a bit more when I had time, but I had no doubt that she had meant what she said. In a way she was just like Jim, for it was he who had told me what seemed such a long time ago to say what you mean and mean what you say. The way she had said it made me want to be happy for her and with her, and I was that.

"Well, Alicia, if he ain't told you so, I do believe I'd say right here and now that Jim is in love with you." For the second time I started to leave the room and was stopped, this time by the sound of a voice.

"Sean."

A glance revealed a young woman who had the look of a schoolgirl who has just kissed her first boy and can't wait to tell her best friend. And who knows, maybe right then I was her best friend.

"Ma'am?"

"He has told me," she said, her smile widening, the flush on her cheeks growing redder. "He said he wants to marry me come spring."

I never will forget the look on her face right then, likely because it struck me that that must be how a woman looks when she falls in love.

They say that ride we made carrying the news of the election of Abraham Lincoln to the presidency was one of the fastest in the Pony's history. The only one faster was when we brought the news of the declaration of war on the South that started the War between the States, but that was down the road a piece yet. Still, that ride was made in seven days, and that was right fast for the Pony.

Rosa got settled in. Alicia and Aaron Stiles made her feel right at home, and she took to the station with no problem at all. The only question that stayed in my mind about Rosa was whether she felt the same about me as Alicia did about Jim. Here I was having these feelings about Rosa, feelings that should have been the same as those Jim held for Alicia, but I couldn't do anything about them, likely because a man didn't do such things as that unless there was marriage in the fore. I reckon it was the way of things. Except there was that one time out at the cave. I had to admit that the whole thing had me mystified now, it purely did. It wasn't that I didn't *want* to sneak into Rosa's room at night, you understand. I just *couldn't*.

By then a new wrangler had been signed on, handpicked by Jim, and he got along well with everyone, including Wash, me, and Rosa. The weather started getting very cool, and a week or so after Rosa had handed out those buffalo robes and legging furs we all had reason to wear them.

One afternoon I was scheduled for a westbound run, and it was cold enough to need extra warmth, so I strapped on those wolfskin furs for the first time since seeing whether they fit and readied myself for my ride. I didn't want to leave the warmth of the fire inside the house, but the rider was due any minute now, so I got up to leave. It was then that Rosa stepped forward to meet me at the door. You'd have thought she was some kind of fancy valet the way she held that robe for me to put on, but that was sure enough what she had in mind.

"You must wear this now," she said, automatically finding my arms for the sleeves. "It is time now." I'd no doubt that the robe was warm, but it sure was heavy, and for a moment I had a notion that it would slow me down. I reckon it showed, too.

"She's right, son," Aaron Stiles said. "Before the day's out, it'll be freezing cold, especially with this wind coming up."

So I wore it, and I do believe it saved my life. Mine and that of my mount.

Some of the horses used by the Pony Express were Morgans, and we rode some breeding animals at the beginning, but by now it was mostly half-broken mustangs that carried us through, and in a way I was glad of it. Oh, a goodly share of them were just as wild as they were broken and a bit hard to handle at first, but they had heart, and no matter what they tell you about a horse's blood line or breeding, they ain't worth spit unless they've got heart. That was one thing I found out for a certainty by the time my ride was through that day. Fact is, it was one thing I never did change my mind about.

It was cold all right, and the wind was picking up just as Aaron Stiles had said it would. The front brim of my hat was plum worn out by then from my taking it off by grabbing hold of the front instead of the top like most folks did. And to tell the truth, I hadn't minded the burning sun or the wind and rain when it beat down, but when the snow started falling like Mother Nature didn't figure on there being any tomorrow, well, hoss, I was wishing for a coonskin cap plain and simple.

I made that ride all right, but by the time I got to the next station it was a full-scale blizzard that was building up out there!

That was when I did something stupid. It seemed awful brave at the time, but looking back I'd say it was stupid. I swung off my mount and pulled off the mochilas I was carrying and looked for the relay pony.

"You'd better get inside till this blows over," a skinny fella said, sticking his head out the cabin door. I could just barely hear him and decided that, for the moment anyway, standing on the lee side of that storm seemed like a good idea. When I asked where the mount I should have was, he pointed to a small wooden building that must have been the barn. I took a step toward the barn and felt a hand on my arm.

"You ain't thinking about getting through this blizzard, are you?" the man said, a look of amazement on his face.

That was when I said something that sounded brave.

"I thought we hired on to deliver the mail,"

I said, acting as brazen as some young squirt trying to make a name for himself.

"You're crazy!" I don't know if it was a look of horror or surprise or stupefaction that came across his face just then, but it's the kind of expression you don't see too often in life.

"Could be," was all I said as I led my mount to the barn, threw myself and that mochila onto an already saddled mustang, and lit out hell for leather like it was any other ride.

But I didn't ride like that for long. The blizzard was soon on me full force, and it was all I could do to keep my hat on with one hand and hold the reins with the other. That was when I started getting kind of scared because it got so bad I couldn't see but fifteen, twenty, thirty yards to my front at the most. I made the mistake of letting a thought pass through my mind just then, and when I did, the fear in me froze me stiffer than the wind. You see, hoss, what crossed my mind just then was that I was lost!

Lost! I'd never been that in my life before, and this was one hell of a time to find out what you need to do!

I dismounted then, not knowing how far I'd come or where I was or what I could do about it. I reckon those are the times in life when you get to thinking about the strangest things. Trouble is, they're usually the *wrong* things to be thinking about. Right then the first thing that hit my mind was that I hadn't stopped for food or coffee or anything back there and was feeling hungry and tired at once. But one thing I knew I had to do was find shelter, and I was fortunate enough at least to do that for myself and the horse. It wouldn't have taken much to beat it, but it got us out of the wind and the face of the driving snow that didn't seem like it would ever end. I didn't recognize that small clump of trees we huddled in, but you can bet I was grateful for them being there just then.

I'd heard the stories about how people had frozen to death in the mountains in such blizzards and snowfalls. Especially the story about the Donner party over in the Nevada Territory back in the winter of '46 when I was born. Some had survived, but the party had turned to cannibalizing one another before it was all over. Well, I wouldn't have to worry about that, for there was just me and my horse, and I figured both of us were too cold to try to eat each other just then. Still, I had to stay awake or I'd be gone beaver. I had to concentrate on how to get out of this mess, how to get the mail through like I'd bragged back there, a brag I was beginning to regret. Lordy, I was getting tired. If I could only sit for a while and think this thing out. What was it that took all the strength out of you so fast? The wind? The cold? The snow? Or was it all three?

Something landed on my leg, and I pulled my head upright. I'd been about to pass out, about to go to sleep. Or had I *been* asleep? And if I had, how long? That may be the only time I ever felt any compassion for those stringy jackrabbits I'd had occasion to kill and eat, for there was one a-sitting on my leg as calm as could be. It was like he knew I was in as much danger as he was, the way he looked at me.

Danger . . .

The thought of it brought me back to the reality of the situation. I got up quickly then and spent I don't know how long stamping my feet and flailing my arms about until I was sure I was wide awake. I was damn cold, but I was awake. I reckon that was what I needed, for I soon found myself overcome by a feeling of calm, a sort of self-assurance that told me I would make it through this ride yet.

The stories I had heard from my brothers

and those who knew them were the only real accounts I knew of how to survive in this wilderness, and oddly enough, it was then I began recalling some of these stories, something in the back of my mind telling me that I would find the answer in them. Both Nathan and Finn had served as Texas Rangers and had been in and out of enough scrapes to last most men five lifetimes. They had fought Indians, Mexicans, Comancheros, and outlaws in general, some of them merely greedy men who had tangled with the wrong man's fortune.

Some of those stories sure enough seemed like tall tales, but I had never questioned my brothers about just how far they might have stretched the truth. It might have been ten minutes or it might have been an hour I spent running over those stories in my mind; I never will know. But finally I had it. What it concerned was the big difference between Nathan and Finn—how Nathan would fight at the drop of a hat and how Finn was always the thinker in the family. I remembered that, and then I thought of Jim for a minute. And then, by God, I had it! It wasn't what Nathan or Finn or Jim did to get them into those fights but what they did once they were in them. Moving, that was it! Whenever they got into a fight, they kept moving, always doing something, even if it was wrong, but always doing *something*! And here I was sitting on my duff wondering what to do. So I moved!

I got on my horse and tied the reins together and held on for dear life . . . and let that horse have his head. If I wandered far enough, maybe I'd ride myself out of this blizzard, though it was still blowing hard. Of course, I might also ride myself over the end of a cliff and die trying to get out of here, but at least I'd be moving, at least I'd be *trying*. But that feeling of confidence rushed over me again, and somehow I knew I'd make it. Not because I was some kind of genius or anything but because I had the common sense to let that old mustang find us the way out. Jim had said they had a good sense of direction, which was true, for hadn't Wash and I passed each other in the night asleep in the saddle as our mounts carried us to our destinations? Then why couldn't the mustang lead me out of this constant whirl of snow that only seemed to get thicker as time went on?

As best I could figure, it was an hour before I got my bearings and spotted what I thought to be a landmark. I got a break then, and the snow lifted some and I made it into a small town a few miles off the route.

"Didn't expect to see anyone out in this weather, son," one of the townsmen said as I pulled up before what looked like an eatery of sorts. "You look pretty well done in to boot." I dismounted and grabbed the mochila, not wanting to lose it after what I'd been through so far. The man must have spotted it too, for he pushed back the door to the restaurant and yelled, "Hank, we got a Pony rider here got off the route some. How 'bout taking his horse down to the livery and get it took care of pronto."

Soon there was another man by my side, taking the reins as I was led into the warmth of the restaurant and toward a table. Before I knew it there was coffee in front of me and a small group of people gathering to ask questions —about the weather, the Pony, and everything that had been happening out in my direction. You'd have thought they didn't have so much as a town newspaper the way they were throwing questions at me. But by the time I had finished my coffee, there was a refill on the way and a huge plate of sliced beef and potatoes was placed before me, along with a basket of homemade rolls. I don't believe I would have answered any questions then if they'd asked, as hungry as I was; I was just hoping my horse was getting fed as well as I was.

When I was through with the meal, I had a renewed sense of energy within me, or maybe I was getting used to the warmth. At any rate, I felt like getting on with what I had to do, and I only answered a few more of the citizens' questions before pushing myself back from the table and picking up the mochila.

"There's a fresh mount for you down at the livery, son," the townsman who had first met me said as I headed for the door.

"What about that mustang I rode in?"

"Oh, don't you worry about him; he's getting cared for good."

"Fine. And thanks for the meal. I'm obliged to you."

"'Tain't nothing, son. We're right proud of what you lads are doing. You just keep it up." He said it with a tone of reverence I'd not heard in a long time, particularly aimed at me.

"Well, now, mister, I'll pass that on to the boys at the other end of the run," I told him. "They'll think kindly of you for saying it."

It almost made the pain I had gone through worth it to hear a small town like that voice such a high opinion of the Pony. There was just one thing that needed changing before I left that town. And that was my horse. I had to have that mustang for the rest of the run. Call it superstition or whatever you will, but that old mustang had heart, and that was what I needed more than a fresh mount right now—a horse with heart. So I resaddled the mustang and lit out on the trail I should have been on in the first place.

The snow was still coming down something fierce, but it wasn't as bad as it had been in the middle of that blizzard. It had lightened up some, enough so that the mount had sight of where he was going. And at times I could even see the landmarks that had been my guide and that were so familiar to me now. It was rough going, hoss, that part of the trip surely was, for I could hear my horse breathing hard above the wind as we made that last sprint into the station that was the end of the line for me. I jumped off the horse and threw the mochila to the new relay rider, who would have no difficulty from now on, for the snow had eased up considerably.

"Two hours late," he said, taking the mochila and mounting up.

"Surprised it ain't more," I said. "One helluva storm back there." I jerked a thumb back over my shoulder to where I'd come from.

"I suspect," he said, and was gone.

A wrangler had taken the mustang and led him away to what I was sure would be a well-deserved rubdown and feeding. Me, I grabbed the cup of coffee that was thrust at me when I entered the cabin, oblivious to the fact that it was scalding.

"Well, I'll be," another man said, eying my outfit. "They finally taught 'em how to dress up for this kind of weather."

I'd all but forgotten about the buffalo robe and the wolfskin leggings and took the time now to undo them, realizing as I did so the tremendous amount of weight I had been carrying from the snow and ice that had clung to the furs and my body.

The coffee was warming me now as a feeling of tiredness came over me. What I needed was sleep and plenty of it. I was about to set the cup down and look around for a bunk to sprawl out in, when the wrangler who had taken my horse entered, a sad look about him.

"Something wrong?"

"He didn't make it, son."

"Huh? What are you taking about?" I asked, puzzled.

"He had heart, son, but he played it all out getting you here. Hate to see a horse go like that." It was an offhand way, the way he said it, not critical or anything, just a statement of fact.

I thought about them then, Rosa and her robes and furs, and that old mustang and his heart. I didn't think about them long, for I was exhausted and in need of rest. But there was one thing I knew for sure, and that was that both of them had saved my life on that ride. And for that much I owed them.

But then, there are some debts I reckon a body don't mind owing.

13

SURVIVING that blizzard gave me a new appreciation of life. But then, I reckon events like that sort of do that to you. It was the same feeling I'd had after coming out of that Indian fight in nearly one piece. Sort of makes a body appreciate what he's got around him, if you know what I mean. Especially the people. Fact is, I got to taking a real close look at what Jim and Alicia meant to each other, and it set me to thinking.

Finally, I made a decision. And when I did, I got to wondering if that wasn't what this growing up business was all about, anyway. Just flat making decisions one day after another. I could remember coming out here with Jim months back and thinking how I *wished* it was this way or that. Now, maybe that's the way it is; maybe taking action makes the difference between a youngster and full growed. I don't know. You'd have to ask Finn or Ma about that; they'd likely know better than me. But I'll tell you what, friend, I was finding it a lot more easy to make decisions now than I had when I first rode into Saint Louis to check on Pa's grave-site.

Mostly, I thought up this plan for Jim's sake. He was like a brother to me, but even if he wasn't, he was still kin, and us Callahans are thick on blood kin relationships. It was going to take some doing, but that didn't make it impossible. So I did some scheming. I had to get Aaron Stiles and Rosa to help me, and Wash when he wasn't riding, but by God I knew we could do it. And believe me, it was hard trying to act like there wasn't a conspiracy going on.

Christmas was only a few weeks away, and that was when I was figuring to unhatch my scheme. At least, I couldn't think of a better season for it. Everything went fine, and it was all set up to happen just as planned. The trouble was, I almost didn't make it.

Wash and I had been making our rides as usual, with little if any trouble from either nature or the Indians. Not that we were getting comfortable with the rides or anything, you understand. Nosirree! After being shot up by Paiutes and damn near frozen to death by Mother Nature herself, you can bet I was on constant lookout for both. But it wasn't either one of them that gave me the trouble I encountered that Christmas Eve afternoon on the last trek of my eastbound ride to the Stiles station house.

It would be late afternoon when I arrived there, giving me enough time to wash up and get ready for the Christmas Eve festivities. The weather had warmed some since the blizzard, although it had snowed off and on. The trail I was following was still an easy one, and I didn't expect trouble, which is exactly what I got. There's a stretch of prairie to the south of the route that is pure flat land and a goodly share to the north that runs into brush country, thick forest, or mountains, depending on where you are. So even if the trail wasn't all that visible for the snow covering it, I still had my landmarks to guide me to my destination. The sun was out and gave a harsh glare to the snow, which is why I didn't see them right off. But most likely, it was because I had my mind on doings at the Stiles house that night. Besides, I wasn't expecting highwaymen.

I don't know where they came from, but it could have been anywhere. I had my mustang going at a pretty good clip, confident that I'd be on time, when my hat flew off my head before I heard the shot that took it off. I looked to the rear and saw two men riding hell for leather at me, guns blazing. If they'd been just sitting, waiting for me all day, it stood to reason that they had fresh mounts, and that made gaining on me right easy. And that I didn't like.

They were feeling right gamy the way the lead was flying through the air, and I determined that if they wanted a fight I'd give them one. But not out in the open like this. I headed that horse of mine off toward a grove of trees, figuring that once I had some cover I'd be able to defend myself. At least, that's what I was going to try to do.

One thing I had found out riding the Pony all that while was that I didn't like being pushed. Hell, there ain't nobody likes being treated like a pile of manure, and I reckon I was finding out that I wasn't any different from the rest. Maybe it was growing pains or trying too hard that made me do what I did next. Jim, I reckon he'd just smile and say it was the Callahan in me, and maybe it was. All I know is that I wasn't but fifteen or twenty yards from that grove of trees when it crossed my mind that those fellas had shot my one and only hat off and I was feeling a mite drafty atop. And, like I'd heard Nathan and Finn and Jim say so often, *that tore it!*

It must have surprised them as much as it did me, for in one split second I had that mustang spun around facing them so fast that if he'd stopped on a dime, he could have given change! And don't ask me how I got it out from underneath that buffalo robe, but by the time my horse and I were facing them, I had that Navy out and commenced to throwing lead at them while I charged them flat out. They didn't seem none too happy about that, especially when I put a slug in one of them's leg. Oh, they'd been shooting at me all the while, but I didn't expect any different by then. Hell, I reckoned it wasn't the mail they were after, *it was me!*

One of them getting hit seemed to take the bite out of them, though. If it hadn't, I'd have been dead meat for sure, for by then I was plumb out of bullets and would have had to do some fiddling to get my other Navy out. I felt something tug at my shoulder as they rode away from me but didn't pay it any attention right off, for I'd gotten a quick glance at them after emptying that Colt of mine. I thought maybe I knew who they were as I walked that horse over to where my hat lay. I saw it had a bullet hole clean through the top, but I put it on anyway. Hell, that's why I'd done what I did, wasn't it?

"Come on, old hoss," I said sticking my heels into the horse's side. "You've had enough of a rest."

I thought about that stunt I'd pulled the rest of the way to the station, and I'll tell you, hoss, it sure didn't seem like the sanest thing I had ever done. After all, taking risks like that over a blame fool hat, why that was . . . well, I don't know what you'd call it except maybe just a bit around the bend. Still, it felt good to be able to face two desperadoes like that without wondering if you were going to die. Then it hit me. I *hadn't* thought about dying like I had that first time with the Paiutes. Had it been reflex action that had made me do what I did? Was I becoming hardened and used to the dangers I knew I'd be facing when I signed on for this job? That was something to think about.

It was the sight of the blood coming from the top of my shoulder as I dismounted that brought the panic to everyone, I reckon. Me, I'd been so deep in thought about what had gone on back there and who was behind it that

I hadn't much noticed the sting I'd felt in the arm in battle or the warm feeling of it as I'd continued my ride.

"Sean, you've been shot!" I heard Alicia yell from the porch as I dismounted—that brought damn near everyone else out of the house, too. I spoke to Wash, who'd be making the ride on the next leg of the trip, while the others gathered around.

"I got ambushed not too far from here, Wash," I said, with the others taking it all in. "I scared 'em off, but keep a lookout, lad, for they may try to get you, too."

"Why do you say that?" he asked, securing the mochila and swinging into the saddle.

"Yeah, who was it?" Aaron Stiles asked, with concern in his voice. But it was Jim I spoke to in answer.

"You remember those two hard cases we ran into back in Saint Joe when Wash and me were just signing up?"

A troubled look came to his face as Jim nodded, remembering the fight and the men. "Rodell and Hardin."

"I think it was them."

"Are you sure, son?" Stiles asked. I could tell by the tone of his voice that he wanted to know just what it was he was getting into. "Couldn't they have been after the mail?"

"Not hardly," I heard myself saying, feeling the same mad I had in that shootout back there on the plains. I pulled my hat off and stuck a finger through the hole. "These fellas was out to kill me."

Wash broke the tension with a chuckle, which got the attention of everyone.

"He's probably right, Mr. Stiles. Them two got a mean streak a mile wide. Besides, I doubt they know how to read, so they couldn't be wanting the mail."

Jim saw the humor in it and smiled, and I reckon Aaron Stiles did too. Or maybe he remembered just what it was we'd been planning for that night and decided to discuss the matter at another time.

"You take care of yourself, Wash," he said, giving me a glance, "just in case young Callahan is right."

After that, Wash was gone, and I got ushered into the house, with Rosa pulling the buffalo robe off my left shoulder as Alicia heated some water. As always, Rosa was silent, speaking only when spoken to or when she thought she had something of value to add to the conversation. Maybe Indian women are like that.

It wasn't more than a flesh wound where the bullet had hit me. Fact is, it took more out of the buffalo robe than it did me. Still, it felt good to get it patched up.

"Here, let me get that, Rosa," Jim said, taking a piece of cloth out of her hand. "Why don't you give Alicia a hand with the supper."

Rosa smiled down at me as she silently walked away, but the look she gave me said she was proud of me, and somehow that was enough to make up for what she might not have said.

"Seems to me you're going out of your way to get shot up just 'bout the time you need a new size shirt, fella." He was in the spirit of the season, I'll say that for Jim, and I was glad, for we had a real surprise laid out for him.

"Could be," I said, "but were I you, I wouldn't belittle these small-caliber guns like my Navy."

"Oh?" He cocked a curious eye toward me.

I pulled out the empty Navy pistol, hefting it in my hand for good measure.

"One of those fellas is carrying a few grains

of my lead in him." That got his attention right quick.

"Well, now, you keep shooting like that and your brothers are going to want you to sign up for the Rangers."

I knew he was having fun joshing me; at least I think he was joshing me about the Texas Rangers and all. On the other hand, like I said, sometimes you couldn't tell about Jim.

Reverend Black showed up right on schedule for supper. Alicia was taken by surprise at having an extra mouth to feed, but there was always plenty of food in the Stiles home. Mr. Stiles gave the excuse that he'd invited the reverend out so that he could talk with him about the wedding that Jim and Alicia were planning for this coming spring. The reverend was one of those tall, reedy fellas I used to see riding the circuit back around Denver. They always looked like they'd never been fed proper, their black frock coats hanging on them like they were skin and bones underneath. Of course, none of them had the reputation—or size—of a man like Peter Cartright, the Methodist fire-eater who'd been preaching on the frontier since before Ma could remember.

It was when Rosa was cleaning the dishes

from the table that the reverend got a mischievous look about him and Jim got to feeling a bit squeamish by the looks of him. I reckon arguing with a man of God was a whole lot worse than arguing with a brace of Colts, especially if you believed what those sky pilots were telling you.

"Now, as I understand it," the reverend began, "you two are ready to commit youselves to each other in marriage."

"Well, uh . . . yes, sir," Jim said, hesitating at first, then reaching across the table to find strength in Alicia's hand. She smiled at him, blushing, and nodded yes, her eyes never leaving his.

"Now, there can't be no doubting, young man." I don't think Jim caught hold of the false seriousness in the preacher's voice just then, he was that taken by Alicia. After a moment of silence, the reverend glanced at Mr. Stiles and me, remarking, "I do believe they're in love." Mr. Stiles smiled, nodding silently while the preacher did some coughing to get Jim and Alicia's attention.

"Yes, sir," Jim said, coming out of his trance. "You were saying."

"I was saying that it might be kind of difficult

for me to make it out this way come spring." A momentary look of despair came to the young couple's faces, although I wasn't quite sure what kind of thoughts might be going through their minds right then. "Be that as it may," the reverend continued, breaking into a smile here, "I doubt it would have made much difference. You see, I came out tonight to marry you *now*."

The preacher was still smiling about the whole thing, but you could have knocked Jim and Alicia over with a feather, they were that stunned!

"No! You can't!" Alicia said. "I'm not ready! I'm—"

"You will be," Rosa said, placing a calm hand on her shoulder. With that she led the frantic girl away to her room.

"Say, who's idea was this, anyway?" Jim said, although I wasn't sure if he was all that pleased with it.

"Well, son, it was Aaron here who persuaded me to leave my own family to do this ceremony on Christmas Eve, but I gather that the idea is the brainstorm of this young man," he said, nodding at me.

"You?"

I shrugged, smiling weakly. "Alicia said she wanted to do for you, and I figured you felt the same for her." I couldn't think of anything else to say and looked to Mr. Stiles for help.

"She's had her cap set for you ever since she saw you, Jim," he said. "Besides, it seems about time that she had a decent Christmas present."

"Well . . . I—" It was the first time I had seen him speechless like this.

"You'd better go get ready, son," Reverend Black said.

"Yeah, I reckon I'd better."

The preacher did the ceremony right in that room. Aaron Stiles got his wife's wedding band out, and I got the reverend to use the Bible I'd been issued as a Pony Express rider so long ago. I reckon it made me feel like I had some part in their marriage. Once they were officially married, it was like one of those family reunions, all sorts of backslapping and women crying and all. Everyone was happy. Aaron Stiles made a place for the preacher to stay overnight, and we even opened up the Christmas presents then instead of waiting until the next morning. I even forgot that Christmas Day was my birthday and that I'd be all of fourteen years old. I don't remember what it was that I got for presents, for it didn't seem to be important anymore.

14

FOR about three months afterwards it was hard finding time to talk to Jim. Hell, it was hard finding Jim! But then, I reckon that's the way married life is. I'll say this for Jim and Alicia, they sure did enjoy getting used to each other. I don't think I ever saw two people more happy with the world . . . and each other. So I took my time with Jim when and where I could, not really pressing him for it. After all, I was the one who had had a hand in his getting married that Christmas Eve.

Wash and I kept busy delivering the mail just like we had for close to a year now. Trouble was that I was getting kind of restless, carrying a notion in my head once in a while that maybe I ought to strike out to somewhere else and make a go of it. I knew Wash was feeling the same thing by the way he acted, which wasn't much different from me, I reckon. I thought about it one day and came to the conclusion that the only thing really holding me back was Jim. Not that I owed Jim anything, you understand, though I was well aware of all he had done for me. But I knew that he'd pass all he had done on to luck or fate or some such thing and not take any credit for it at all. It was his way. But married or not, I had come to consider Jim as my saddle pard, not just kith and kin but one to ride the river with, a man I could count on.

"You feel like taking a break?" he asked me one day out at the corrals. He was still in good spirits nearly all day, and I had a suspicion he'd be looking and feeling that way for the rest of his life, as long as Alicia was there. Seeing him like that made me feel good about that fixing up I'd done with Aaron Stiles and all at Christmas.

"What do you mean take a break?" It wasn't expected that you would take a break or anything else you might call it with the Pony Express. There was continual work to be done from can see to can't see, and you were expected to pick up the slack where it was needed, so I reckon his comment sort of threw me.

"Oh, I was just thinking," he replied, shrugging, "that you got a few days coming and we got us a couple new riders coming in. Thought maybe you'd like to take a ride on back to Saint

Joe and help me bring out a remuda I'm supposed to string out along the route."

It was just what I wanted! But you didn't show emotion out here. That much I'd found out. That was all kid stuff. Yesirree.

"Well, uh, you sure you can spare me?" I tried to sound as serious and calm as possible, all the time feeling my insides asking my head when we were going to saddle and ride.

"Well, I reckon I could always ask Wash—"

"When do we leave?"

I just couldn't fool him, that was all there was to it. He stood there grinning from ear to ear, knowing how badly I wanted to go along. Like I said, Jim was one you could count on.

"Tomorrow soon enough?"

"You bet."

You'd have thought they weren't going to see each other for a couple of years rather than a couple of weeks, the way they made a big deal out of kissing each other the way they did. It wasn't exactly heard of back then to be kissing or even holding hands with a woman in public. I reckon the idea was that love was a private affair and ought to be kept that way. And maybe in them big cities like Saint Joe and

Saint Louis it was, but out here in the wilderness Jim and Alicia paid no never mind to it, not even with Mr. Stiles, Rosa, and me standing there watching.

"Rosa, look after her," Jim said, climbing up in his saddle. The older woman smiled silently, knowing what he meant. "We won't be gone but two weeks at the outside, Aaron. Weather ought to be warming up some by then."

"You're the ones need to be careful," Stiles said. "We got enough guns and ammunition to hold off an army here. But you keep an eye to your sides and back, coming and going. I've a notion we're likely to see Indian activity sometime soon, and if that weather eases up like you predicted, it'll be all the sooner."

"Hurry back, darling," Alicia said, a sad smile on her face that said she was missing him already. "Take care of him, Sean. Don't let him do anything foolish."

"Yes, sir, ma'am," I said it, giving a half-assed salute to the woman standing before me, but she knew it was in jest and laughed.

"Be back as soon as we can," Jim said, and jerked the reins of his horse. I reckon sometimes goodbyes are hard.

We didn't ride hell for leather like I'd been

used to. Then again, we didn't take our lazy old time, either. It was good to be able to ride a horse at an easy pace and not have to wonder if he would drop out from under you for all the strain you put him through. Fact is, the whole trip was sort of quiet, with Jim thinking about Alicia and me just thinking.

It was almost a year now that I'd been riding the Pony, and I found myself wondering what else there was out in the world, out in the West. There was talk of war between the North and the South, of course, but that had been going on ever since I'd joined the Pony. Besides, what could I do in such a war? I had no desire to be a soldier for either side and had given even less thought to why such a war would be fought. Perhaps I was too embroiled in my own world to ponder such things. But more likely it was a matter of trying to keep alive long enough to make my next ride. There simply hadn't been enough time to think about anything but getting the mail through.

The Pony Express wouldn't be around much longer by all indications, either. From the start we riders had been aware of the telegraph poles and wires being strung along the same routes we were riding, all of us knowing that one more pole meant one less day of the Pony. California now had a telegraph that stretched from San Francisco to Sacramento and then some, and it too was being built at a rapid pace. So maybe it was good to be thinking of other things. A body had to look to the future, and doing for yourself was the only way things got done out here.

"Place sure has changed," Jim said as we rode into Saint Joe that fourth day. And he was right. There seemed to be more bustle to the town, more going on than when I'd first arrived here nearly a year ago. The first noticeable change was the carrying of arms by most men. I knew from hearing past accounts that Kansas and Missouri had been hotbeds of resistance in the dispute over slavery, but I didn't think the war would be starting in either of those two territories. You couldn't prove it by looking at the local male population, though. Over half of them were armed to the teeth, some carrying at least two pistols and as many long guns besides. They were gearing for war all right; I found myself saying a silent prayer that they'd not start the shooting until Jim and I were out of town.

"How long'd you say we were going to be

here?" I asked, still taking in the massive amount of arms being carried about.

"No more'n two days if I can find this Roberts character. He's supposed to have the remuda ready and waiting for us." Maybe I was looking more worried than I should have been. If I was, Jim noticed it. He seemed to notice just about everything. "I know you got spoiled on Alicia's cooking, but what say we get us a decent meal before we get to them horses," he said, pulling to a halt in front of a local eatery.

They served beefsteak and potatoes and homemade bread with plenty of coffee for twenty cents a meal, which was kind of high when you considered that the average man wasn't making but less than a dollar a day. But Jim didn't seem to mind the price and insisted on paying for the meal, so I enjoyed it.

That meal was about as silent as any on our trip had been, and I thought that once in a while I spied Jim studying me out of the corner of his eye. What he had in mind I didn't know, and I wasn't about to ask.

It was well into the afternoon by the time we'd finished our meals, found the man, Roberts, and squared away the deal with the remuda Jim and I would move west. After you work with horses for a while you get so you can tell about them at a glance. I'd heard Nathan say that you could tell what a man was about if you watched his eyes, and I reckon that in the same way I'd learned to spot good horseflesh when I first laid eyes on it. And, friend, these were good horses. Feisty to be sure, but nothing I'd ever turn away for riding stock. Besides, it was that feistiness, I'd found out, that gave a horse bottom, gave him heart. And without that there wasn't one worth spit to my way of thinking. Jim made all the necessary arrangements for the time and place to pick up the horses, and that left the rest of the day to us. At least that was what I thought as we walked away from the corral, heading back toward the center of town.

Did you ever notice how easy you can pick a person out of a crowd if you know them? They could be your best friend or just a casual acquaintance . . . or someone you'd never forget, especially someone who'd tried to do you in.

It wasn't that they were all that ugly, unless you counted their dispositions. And as crowded as Saint Joe's main street was that day, I might have missed spotting Rodell and Hardin altogether had it not been for the fact that Hardin was favoring his right leg.

I stopped dead in my tracks in the middle of the street, placing a hand on Jim's arm as I did. And you know something, friend? I do believe that if that street had been full of wagons, I'd have gotten run right over, for all I could see just then was Rodell and Hardin heading for one of the saloons.

"We got trouble," I said, not taking my eyes from the two for a minute.

"No," Jim said, and I turned to see the crooked smile on his face as he recognized them as well. "They're the ones who're in trouble."

We must have both been thinking along the same lines, for Jim started walking toward that saloon the same time that I did, following Rodell and Hardin. Something had changed since I'd last been inside a saloon a year ago, and that was the strange looks we'd gotten when Wash and I had walked in. I didn't have the buffalo robe on any longer, it having warmed up some since we'd ridden out from the station house. That left the two Navy Colts sitting there on my hips, butts forward in full view for everyone to see. I'd grown accustomed to wearing two by now, having left the long gun the Pony had issued behind some time back. It shouldn't have made any difference to see me enter the saloon like that, what with all the extra hardware I'd seen around town when we rode in, but it did. Maybe those who saw me walk in knew how to read a man by his eyes too, for I had an urge to kill right then like I'd never known before. And if it showed, well, so be it.

The ruffians were bellied up to the bar, with two empty spaces on their left side. Jim and I took them, and Jim ordered whiskeys for both of us. By the time the barkeep set the drinks on the counter, Rodell and Hardin had taken a glance at us in the mirror over the bar. Now, I don't know what Jim would have said or done, but I was just too flat mad to stand that peacefully next to those two would-be killers. And you can bet I wasn't waiting for Jim to start the ball.

"You know, Jim," I said, glancing at him and then into the mirror at the faces of the two next to me, "I never was much of a drinker. Against the company policy and all you know."

That was when I tossed the whiskey into Hardin's face and brought the back of my other hand across his jaw as I pushed him back. It surprised me that the blow staggered him, and I wasted no time in giving him another. A lot of those barkeeps still made their own home brew, using straight grain alcohol and a tincture of this and that to liven it up, and I'd heard Nathan talk about how it could blind a man if he drank too much of it. Well, hoss, it seemed to me right then that this whiskey was doing a good job of blinding Hardin, even without his being drunk, for he could only rub his eyes as I hit him again hard in the face, felling him.

I needn't have worried about Rodell, the bigger one, for as soon as I'd stepped out of the way, Jim had caught him with a roundhouse left full in the face while the man was going for his gun.

"Take it outside," the barkeep said, brandishing a scattergun from what seemed like nowhere. His voice was the only one to be heard, since all eyes were upon Jim and me and the two thugs on the floor. Hardin was getting some of his vision back now as he got up on one knee and gave me an ugly glare. Then he rose unsteadily to his feet.

"I should have taken you last year when I had the chance," he said.

"I wish you'd tried," I heard myself saying,

which seemed to surprise me more than anyone else.

Hardin would have gone for his gun if the bartender hadn't had that shotgun at the ready, so I hit him again, full in the face, unexpectedly. He staggered back again toward the door, not knowing I could hit that hard, I reckon. Hell, I didn't know I could hit that hard either! I found myself hammering away at his face, the pain in my knuckles not mattering at all, for I knew that the pain he was feeling must surely be worse. I'd completely lost track of what Jim and Rodell were doing, concentrating on the man with the game leg as I pushed him backwards out the door.

Something caught my eye then, a distraction I wasn't ready for, and I had the oddest feeling as I tried to adjust my sight to the figure across the street. But he must have seen me look and was gone in a second, and that was more than enough time for Hardin to get in his licks. A fist drove into my side, and I had the immediate urge to sink to the broadwalk boards, catching hold of the side of a windowpane for support. For one split second I couldn't see him for the pain I was feeling, but I knew approximately where he was and lashed out at him with a wild left hand.

It hit his shoulder, and I saw him go for his pistol again, when he was stopped by the huge body of Rodell, who bumped right into him on the way out of the saloon. The big man knocked Hardin to the side, and I caught him full in the brisket with a hard right as he staggered against the roof support. It knocked the wind out of him, and then I hit him again, sending him into the street in a puddle of mud, where Rodell fell atop him.

I didn't know if it was my side or my fist that hurt more or even if I was still capable of drawing a pistol for that matter, but I didn't really give a damn right then.

Those who had been watching inside the saloon had followed the fight outside and were now part of the crowd that had gathered around us.

"All right, break it up," a tall, lanky man with a sheriff's badge on his vest said as he appeared before us. "What caused it this time?" he wanted to know. "Another argument about states' rights?"

"More like the right to die, Sheriff," Jim

said, rubbing his fist. "You see, I never took to anyone trying to do in my kin."

"What about you?" he asked, looking at me.

"I'm the one they tried to kill," I told him.

"Where'd this all take place?" I got the impression that he was sort of bored with the whole thing, that he figured he had better things to do. When I told him how they'd tried to bushwhack me on my Pony Express route, he looked down at the two men coming to now, and then back at Jim and me. "That's out of my jurisdiction, so I can't help you none on that. And the US marshal's out of town for another week or so, and to tell you the truth, fellas, I'm just plain tired of all this fighting that goes on every hour on the hour." Rodell and Hardin were aware of what was going on now, and he included them in the conversation as well. "You've got some kind of feud going on, you settle it amongst yourselves. But all four of you have got one hour to get out of town." He pulled a watch out of his pocket fob and opened it. "And you just wasted five minutes of it. Now, *do I make myself clear?*" The way he said it, you'd have thought he could have killed all four of us and then some right on the spot.

"We got everything we came for, Sheriff," Jim said. Then, looking down on the ruffians, his voice changed from the peaceable one he'd used with the sheriff to one of downright meanness. "Mister, that's the second time I've had a run-in with you. I reckon the third time ought to be a charm. If you got any smarts, you'll stay away for good."

"That a threat?" Rodell wasn't speaking too well now, what with the blood coming out of his mouth and being minus a couple of teeth. Still, he made himself known.

"Hell, no!" Jim replied. "My pa used to say he never made a threat in his life, just claimed he gave fair warning."

The big man chuckled. "That what you say, sonny?"

"Nope. I figure by the time I'm through with you, you'll be guarding the back gates of hell. But mister, you ain't going to be doing it in one piece. I'll guarantee that!"

Jim turned to leave, and I did the same, but first I stopped and once again faced Hardin.

"You come within shooting range of me, *friend*, and you won't just wind up with a gamy leg." He started to smile, and I backhanded him across the face, letting him know I didn't fear him. "You sorry bastard, I'll shoot your goddamn kneecaps off. And that's guaranteed, too!"

Jim was saddling up at the livery when I got there. I saddled my mount in silence before Jim spoke up.

"You mind telling me why you started that fight?"

I smiled at him, feeling good for all the pain various parts of my body were going through at the moment. "Hell, Alicia said I was to take care of you."

"You? Take care of me? That'll be the day!" He said it in a blustery manner, and I wasn't sure if he was joshing me like he did at times or if he was serious. But I knew he meant it when he looked across his saddle at me and said, "For what it's worth, you done right fine back there, Sean. Better'n I figured. I'm proud of you."

I noticed something then that I hadn't noticed before. It was like something you stick in the back of your mind but forget to bring to the fore again. And just then it hit me. And when I saw a strange look come into Jim's eyes, I had the feeling that the same notion had crossed his mind too. Then, slowly, we both walked out around our mounts and took each other in from top to bottom. It was the damndest thing you ever saw!

"By God, I was right!" he said, and suddenly I knew what it was he had been studying about me on the trail, something that I'd completely overlooked. "Boy, you done some growing in the past year!"

And he *was* right. I recalled having to look up to him whenever I was talking to him back when we first started out on the Pony. I must have grown four or five inches since then, for now I was looking Jim straight in the eye, and Jim was a good six foot plus! Suddenly the shirt I wore felt a smidgen too tight, and I felt myself blush, not knowing what to do. Or say.

"Unless you ain't been told, Sean, you turned into quite a man," he said, climbing up into his saddle. "Fact is, you ain't been a boy for some time now. Reckon it takes a good fandango like that one back there to bring it out in a body." He was silent for a moment before saying, "I reckon we'd better get that remuda before the sun sets. We can get some time in the saddle 'fore it's time to make camp."

There were fifty head of horses, and we got them as quickly as we could and lit out of that town before any more trouble could start that we'd get blamed for. It was getting close to sunset when we found a stream and let the horses water before making camp. Jim had had a silly grin on his face ever since leaving the livery, and I couldn't figure out what it was for. Fact is, it wasn't until we got the horses settled for the night that I found out. He rode up beside me, looking me up and down as though disbelieving what he saw.

"Ma ain't going to believe this," he said with a chuckle.

"Huh?"

"Why, shoot, boy, you're a Callahan!" He said it with the pride one brother has for another when they've both come out of a fight like we had.

"I thought I always was," I said, a bit bewildered.

"Yeah," he said, still smiling. "There's that too."

15

IT took a day or two to get the surprise of being a full-grown man to wear off, but I didn't have much time to think about it, what with the remuda keeping both Jim and me busy from can see to can't see. And he was right about the weather warming up, for about the third day it seemed that the farther we went, the less snow we were seeing, unless it was hidden in a grove of trees or somewhere. We tied up those buffalo robes during the day and used them for covers at night when it cooled off and the fire went out, figuring that they'd be of little use until next winter.

Since our visit had been cut short, we had plenty of time to get back to the Stiles house within the two-week limit Jim had set for us, so we sort of took our time visiting the relay stations along the way and dropping off a specified number of horses at each. I reckon we spent a goodly share of our evenings at those relay stations telling the people employed there what was going on in the rest of the world; it surprised me how much interest and tension was building up concerning the North and the South and their differences. It was the fourth day out that the fight and what had happened there in Saint Joe came back to my mind in full, and I remembered something I'd completely forgotten until then.

"You keep frowning like that and you're going to look as serious as Pa down at San Jacinto," Jim said with a smile. "And I hear he had a fearsome look about him that time."

I didn't want to ruin his good disposition, but if he wanted to know what was bothering me, well, I'd tell him. Besides, I'd no wish to keep it to myself any longer.

"You recall that fight we got into back there?" I said, jerking my thumb over my shoulder.

"Yeah, why?"

"Well, once I got Hardin out of that saloon, I would have done him in proper were it not for something I saw out of the corner of my eye. That was when he busted me in the ribs good and hard."

"So . . . what are you talking about?"

I looked him straight in the eye when I told him.

"Across the street, while we were fighting, there was a man standing off by his lonesome."

"Oh?" His smile was gone, replaced by a serious look as he gave the subject new interest. "Recognize him?"

"He was short and sawed off, and he didn't wear a hat like most do," I said, already seeing fear come into Jim's eyes. "I only got a quick look at him, Jim, but I'd swear it was the Cajun."

He swallowed hard, nearly frozen in the saddle, and I thought that if the whole herd took off and disappeared, he'd never have cared. It was Alicia he was thinking about now, and I knew without asking that the only words running through his mind right now were the threats that Cajun and Reitz had made to me and Wash as they left. I'd never have told him about them if Alicia hadn't been standing there along with us when they made the threats; but knowing how Jim felt about her, I had told him anyway. Now, with all that had happened, it looked like I'd rattled him more with that one sentence than any gunfight or fistfight he'd ever been in. Call it fear or terror or love for another that makes a man get that look about him, but Jim had it. I only hoped it wasn't catching.

Suddenly, I had the notion that it well might be catching, for I could feel the same fear and concern well up inside of me for Rosa as I had seen on Jim's face. I couldn't explain it—or maybe I could and didn't want to admit it—but all of a sudden I found myself fearing for Rosa's safety as much as for the Stiles's. I'm sure it showed on my face, although Jim said nothing about it.

The rest of the day he was acting like a gopher at a rattlesnake convention, he was that skittish. He took to silence, which wasn't his nature, even when I tried to assure him that I might have been mistaken. It was Jim who decided that we ought to get the horses doled out as quickly as we could and get back to the Stiles house as fast as our mounts could carry us. Not that I disagreed with him.

The next morning we dropped off the last of the horses at a way station about twenty miles from the Stiles house, it being our last stop of the trek. Fact is, that was the day everything happened.

Everything in the whole world. Or at least it seemed like it.

Jim had just gotten the horses counted and settled into the corral, and he was giving the instructions he'd received to pass along to each relay station. You'd have thought the whole world was going to fall off the edge of a cliff the way that Pony rider came pouring into camp. He must have been as excited as his horse, the way he was panting, and I reckon that got Jim even more excited and worried than he already had been, for a look of concern was soon covering his face.

"What is it, boy?" the manager of the place said. But the lad who was riding in didn't even notice him or me and Jim there. His only concern was for the rider who was taking his place on the route.

"It's Paiutes!" he said, nearly out of breath. "The Stiles station back yonder. They said the word's out the Paiutes is on the warpath again! I hope you got eyes in back *and* the front of you, hoss, cause you're going to need 'em!"

With that the fresh Pony rider was gone as the boy before us got his wind.

"Who told you that?" Jim said, stepping forward. He wasn't asking a question, he was demanding information.

"Mr. Stiles, back yonder," the lad said, throwing a thumb over his shoulder in the direction from which he'd come.

"Were they all right? Stiles? The woman?"

"Yes, sir," the boy said, fearful of what Jim might do if the answer wasn't what he wanted. I could tell that much by the look on both their faces. "They were doing just fine. It's just that Mr. Stiles seemed to be getting kind of nervous about those Injuns on the warpath again."

Jim looked at me hard as the boy and the station manager went into the cabin, but I knew what was on his mind.

"Come on, Jim," I said, trying to sound encouraging, even if I wasn't feeling that way. "Aaron said he had an arsenal of weapons and enough guns and powder to hold off a good attack. You ain't going to let a few Paiutes worry you, are you?"

"First off, Sean," he said in as serious a manner as I'd heard him speak in all week, "there ain't no such a thing as a *good* attack. People always wind up getting themselves killed one way or another." He pulled out his Dragoon now, checked the loads, and added the sixth cap to give him six beans in the wheel. Then he reholstered the pistol and glanced down at me again, still dead serious. "Second, an extra gun never hurt no one. You coming or not?"

It didn't take but a second for him to pull the reins on his mount, dig his heels into the horse, and light out of there like there wasn't any tomorrow. And it didn't take more than that split second for me to make up my mind. By God, Jim had said I was a Callahan, and like I said, us Callahans are thick on family. Besides, Alicia was family now, too, so I followed as fast as I could.

I never could understand how Jim, as big as he was, had gotten the mail through, finishing my route the day I'd gotten shot up by the Paiutes, but I found out that afternoon. He knew how to get everything he needed out of the horse he was riding and spent the better part of the afternoon just out of my sight at the edge of the western skyline. And let me tell you, friend, I'd gotten to be a pretty good hand at riding a mustang by then. I remember realizing that it must not have been anything more than *do* that got Jim through on that ride; he just had to *do* it, and that was all there was to it. Just like his pa would have said, "Don't say it, do it!" And by God, he did, with me trailing him just out of sight.

One thing you learned riding the Pony like I did, and that was that any distance could be the longest one you'd ever have to travel, be it one mile or one hundred. Everything depended on the circumstances of the ride, and that afternoon the twenty miles sure did seem like a long ride. But I knew we were near when I heard the gunshots coming from the Stiles place. It was about the same time I saw Jim pull his mount to a halt, giving me enough time to catch up to him.

"You're getting slow, boy," was all he said as I pulled to a halt beside him. He didn't look at me; his glare was fixed on the station house as he checked the loads on the second Dragoon he kept in his slicker. There was murder in his eyes, and by the time I saw what he had seen, I felt the same way.

There below us, at the bottom of the rise, were four men, four *white* men, laying siege to the Stiles place! It wasn't Paiutes that were doing the raiding this time, although I'm sure it was meant to look that way. It was the four meanest bastards I'd ever come across in my life: Rodell, Hardin, Reitz, and the Cajun!

"Let's see you do to them what you done to them Paiutes, Sean," Jim said. "I'm going to come at 'em from the north side. You see if you can get their attention with them Navys of yours."

And then he was gone.

He hadn't told me what he wanted me to do, and I took it as a sign of faith in my knowing instinctively. Nathan had said our pa had been fighting since whoever flung the first chunk, and right now seemed about as good a time to find out if that ran in the family blood too.

I lit down into them like some crazy Comanch' that'd been liquored up good on Taos Lightning, so they heard me coming before I was in pistol range. That gave them a chance to start throwing lead at me before I could get to them, but it also gave me the edge of having more lead to throw back at them when I did get in range.

If I got in range!

I was just about there when I caught a slug in my left arm, throwing me back some in the saddle. I don't know if it was something I did that made the mustang come to a halt right then or if it was the gunfire that was erupting from everywhere, but that's exactly what he did. I was maybe thirty yards from the house now, but it was close enough for me, so I slid off the horse and tried dodging bullets while throwing some of my own as well. If that wasn't enough racket to get their attention so that Jim could come at them from the north side, I didn't know what was. I plinked a shot off at Reitz as he ran for his horse but missed him, hitting the horse in the head and killing him instantly. If I'd had time, I would have felt bad about that, for I'd never killed a horse on purpose. But the gunfire kept me moving, and I found myself wondering where in the hell Jim was. Where was he?

Rogers, the new man who'd been hired on as a wrangler before we left, was making a run for it from the barn, and he went down. He was hit, sure enough, but I'd no idea if he was dead or just wounded until I saw him make a feeble attempt to reach for his pistol an arm's length away.

Behind him came Aaron Stiles with nothing more than his Hawken in hand. He must have been figuring to make a last stand then and there, for he simply stopped, took a stance, and raised his rifle at one of the men. The Hawken didn't go off until the Cajun's knife had landed in Stiles's chest, knocking him backward as he pulled the trigger. He was dead before he hit the ground.

And if hell hadn't taken a holiday by then, it sure did now as I heard the big boom of Jim's Dragoons being fired as fast as he could pull the triggers. But he must have been firing wild, for he sure wasn't hitting anyone, and that wasn't like Jim at all. But then I saw what had caught his attention, and I reckon I couldn't believe it either.

Alicia came charging out the door with a scattergun in her hand and, aiming at nothing but what was in front of her, pulled both triggers. The sound was deafening, and I thought I saw the Cajun and Reitz flinch some as though they were taking in some of the pellets. There was a terrified look on Alicia's face, and I soon saw it on Jim's as Rodell took dead aim and shot her in the chest. To tell the truth, I don't think Jim even heard that shotgun go off, he was watching Alicia and her actions so intently. But it did something to him, for all of a sudden he was running to her, not even aware of the gunfire that still filled the air.

They would have killed him, I think, if it hadn't been for Rosa stepping into the doorway with a Hawken and shooting another of their horses right between the eyes. A chunk of wood flew out of the door beside her, and she ducked back inside.

We should have *all* been dead! They could have taken us *all*! But once you get past the Mississippi, you find out an old saying that is as true as the sun rising in the east, and that is that a man without a horse ain't nothing. And with two of their horses down, and them knowing what Jim and me could do to them, I reckon they got a bit cautious then. It's the only thing I could figure! There they were, still snapping shots at me while they mounted up two each to a horse and hightailed it out of there. It was the damndest thing I'd ever seen! But then, there seemed to be a lot of that taking place of late.

I rushed to Rogers's side to see how he was doing. He was bleeding from the upper chest but didn't seem any the worse for it. Rosa was running up to me then, and I remembered that my arm had a fiery feeling to it. There was blood running down my sleeve, but the only thing on my mind just then was the sight of Jim holding Alicia in his arms.

"Take care of him," I said to Rosa, motioning toward the fallen wrangler, and went to Jim's side.

"I wanted to do so much for you, Jim," I heard her say as a trickle of blood ran down the side of her mouth and the pool of blood on her clean, white dress took on the shape of some spreading ogre I'd never want to see again.

"You did, honey, you did. You did just fine." His voice wasn't firm now at all, but shaky and fearful; he knew that what had once been his was now almost out of his grasp.

Her hand went to his shoulder, and she squeezed what she could get hold of. There was no more terror in her face now, only the same fear of loss that Jim had, the same knowledge.

"I love you so," was the last thing she said before her head fell to the side. Then, blood and all, he pulled her to him and held her close, whispering in her hair, "I know, I know. I love you too." He held her like that for what seemed like a long time, rocking her back and forth the way you would a baby that can't sleep.

"Come, I must tend to you." It was Rosa who took hold of my arm now, motioning for me to enter the house.

"No," I said, sitting down on the porch. "You'll do it out here." Again she obeyed without question, returning in a few minutes with water and cloth and something to bandage me with. I reloaded our guns while she did what she could to patch me up, watching Jim in silence. By the time she was through, so was I, with both the Navys and Dragoons being fully loaded. What would happen next I didn't know, but the thought of it scared me.

"They killed her," Jim said when he finally looked up, gently laying his wife on the floorboards. He said it as a simple fact, but I could tell by his look it was more than that. "The sonsabitches *killed* her!" This time it was louder, and what I had feared was now coming true. No more would there be the smiling, joshing Jim I had grown to know so well. They had taken the one thing, the one person in his life, he had really loved. And that was unforgivable. And they would pay—*dearly*. But so would Jim. I had seen a hardness come to his eyes, and I felt sure he would never again be the easygoing man I'd known. He wasn't shaking like a man will when he's going to pieces. He was as calm as ever, and it was the calm that scared me, for now Jim Callahan was going to turn the hunters into the hunted. And it was he who would be the cold, determined killer who would make them pay.

With their lives.

Still, he was Jim Callahan, and he might as well have been my brother, and I would follow him to them and exact that same revenge.

"You coming with me?" he asked, picking up both Dragoons and checking the loads. It was a needless question.

"Wouldn't have it any other way," I said, and we saddled up fresh mounts and rode.

16

THERE'S only one run I refused to make in the time I was with the Pony Express, the one I should have run that day, and it wasn't because I had a piece of lead in me.

Wash Bernard came through slumped over in his saddle just as we were leaving. His whole side was bloodied, and the first thing that came to mind was that the Paiutes actually were on the warpath. But there were no arrows, no knives or tomahawks stuck in him like you'd expect, for the Indians had few of the white man's firearms in those days. Both Jim and I eased him out of his saddle, laying him on the ground.

"What happened?" I asked, fearful that I already knew the answer.

"Cajun . . . Reitz . . ."

"Rodell and Hardin," Jim spat out, the words sounding as if they were poison. "They're hateful men, those four. But I clean forgot about you doing any riding today. How did it happen?" There was a tone in his voice now that said he knew what had happened; he only wanted Wash's confirmation.

"They came . . . out of nowhere," Wash blurted out in what sounded like as much surprise and confusion as I was feeling myself. I reckon it showed right then too, for there was pure hatred in Jim's eyes as he looked up at me.

"Like I said, they're hateful men . . . and they ain't wanting to leave *anyone* at the Stiles station alive." Looking at Wash, he added, "They ambushed you good, son."

"Never did get to be a man," the dying boy said, a saddened look on his face as he coughed up blood.

"You listen to me, Wash Bernard," Jim said, looking him right in the eye. He was dead serious, and I knew he wasn't lying when he spoke. "You and Sean and the rest of you youngsters became men a helluva long time ago. You was just never in one place long enough to be told so."

"Really?" He was fading now, but he could still hear Jim.

"That's right, pard." Jim held the boy's hand as he said, "And I ain't lied to you yet."

"No." Wash sort of smiled before his head

rolled to the side, and I thought I had an idea of what Jim must have felt when Alicia died. Now we both had a reason for revenge, and for one fleeting instant it crossed my mind that I might be on the verge of turning out like I figured Jim would. But to tell you the truth, right then I didn't give a tinker's damn.

I yelled for Rosa, and she came running, and that's when I made my decision. The mail and Russell, Majors, and Waddell could wait. I had unfinished business that needed tending to, and it was going to be done before the sun set. I left instructions with Rosa to have the next rider through make some kind of arrangements for getting the mail back on schedule and to send her some help quickly.

"And you?" She had that stoic look on her face, the one that asks a question even when it knows what the answer is.

"I reckon there's some things a man *can't* get out of," was all I could think to say. It may not have been the right thing but it was the truth, and that's what counted. That's what always counted.

We were tracking them for maybe half an hour before I noticed Jim and his coughing. He had paled some, and at first I thought it was the shock of his wife's death. But when I reined in and grabbed his reins, I saw it for certain.

"You damn fool!" I said angrily. It was the first time I'd ever spoken to him in that tone of voice, but after what we'd been through, it didn't seem to phase either of us now.

What I was cussing myself about was all that blood on his shirt! Here I had thought it was from holding Alicia the way he had, getting her blood all over him. And I reckon some of it was hers. But Judas Priest! He had taken a slug high in the chest the same as Rogers, and he was still going! About then I felt myself hating him and admiring him at the same time. He was a damn fool for not getting his wound looked after before we left; he might be dying! Yet there was the part of me that felt a deep pride to be riding with a man who only had one thing in mind—and that was to *do*!

"Ain't got time for no nursing, boy," he said, seeing that I'd noticed his wound. "So don't sass me."

The anger in me came out then, and I reached across him, grabbing his shirt in one hand and damn near pulling him out of his saddle. With the other hand I undid my neckerchief and stuffed it inside his shirt to stifle the bleeding. There was no stopping him, and I had no desire to, not at all. Fact is, that wasn't what I was angry at. But that didn't keep me from talking through gritted teeth when I said, "I'd hate to call you a son of a bitch, Jim, but I sure am getting tired of being called a boy."

I pushed him back upright in his saddle, and for the first time since we'd gotten news that the Paiutes were on the warpath, I saw him smile at me. He was in pain, but it was a smile.

"Like I told Wash back there, you youngsters was full growed some time back." He coughed and spat to the far side, away from me, and I found myself wondering if it was blood he was coughing. When he looked back at me, the laughter was gone and once again there was the hardness of a killer in his eyes. "Seems to me we took this ride with a purpose that didn't have much to do with your growth." When I said nothing, he added, "Then let's get to it."

They were riding double, so they couldn't have gotten that far. And they made no effort to hide their tracks, none at all. It was as if they were waiting for us to come, knew we would, two-to-one odds or not. Strange thing was, it didn't bother me how many there were. It was the spring of the previous year when I'd had my first real encounter with death, when I got shot out of the saddle by those Paiutes. I had been outnumbered and scared to death, figuring I would die on the spot. But I'd made it with Jim's help. And I reckon that what I was doing now was repayment for that . . . as well as a touch of revenge for killing Wash Bernard. And you know something? I had some scared in me, for I reckon that's natural. But what I had more of was *mad*. Not crazy mad, like I seen in Jim's eyes, but flat out tired of being pushed mad. And I wasn't afraid of facing death this time either.

It took another half hour to track them to where they'd left the horses next to a grove of trees. There must have been all of fifty feet of walking distance to the space between those trees and a sharp rock formation that shot straight up into the sky, it seemed. Both of us knew they were likely setting up an ambush for us, but like I said, it was a day for surprises. Dismounting from our own horses, we had another one.

There was a fella by the name of Cullen Baker back then who was gaining a reputation as somewhat of a fast gun. Fact is, there was a fella they called Langford Peel out in Virginia

City who had the same sort of reputation. I didn't know much about either of them except that they made their living by the gun. I reckon they were the first of what you'd call gunmen except that they were a bit before their time, for it wasn't until after the war that so-called gunfighters began showing up on the frontier. You could say that Baker and Peel were the first of their trade to face their opponents in the streets so that everyone could see how fair the fight was when they shot it out with someone. So I reckon you could say I got thrown by the whole thing when we got off them horses and started walking into what we thought was a trap, an ambush, and saw what we did.

Jim was on my left, and from his left side appeared the Cajun and Rodell, the man who had killed Alicia. From my right, out from behind some trees, came Reitz and Hardin, the one with the gamy leg. They were fifty, maybe sixty feet away from us, which could make the situation doubtful when it came to pistol accuracy, at least for snap shooting. It was also enough to send a chill down my spine, and a moment's worth of doubt went through me as I remembered the pain in my side and my arm, wondering how it would affect my shooting.

Then I remembered Alicia and Wash dying that same day, and, just like Jim, it didn't matter how much pain I was in anymore as long as we finished it. That was what mattered.

"Come ready to die, did you?" It was Rodell who spoke first, sounding cocky as all hell.

It was Jim he was talking to, only I couldn't understand how Jim could bleed like he was doing and still stand tall like nothing had happened to him. He was pale in the face, but it wasn't from being scared, you can bet on that.

"Been ready to die for some time now," was all he said. I had a notion he was the one who wanted to start the fandango, but to my surprise it was me that did it. It wasn't none of that stuff you read about good guys and bad guys and who drew first and who was fair about it. That's hogwash! We were dealing with survival here, and fairness had left the game one hell of a long time ago!

"Chillern!" Hardin said, spitting it out harshly.

And that tore it! By God I was a *man*, and this pilgrim was going to know it before he died!

I reached for my Navy, and I reckon everyone else started going for some kind of gun too. But right then I was concerned with Hardin. Now, hoss, I never claimed to be all that fast, but I'm usually accurate, and I was that day, too. I shot Hardin in the left kneecap. It wasn't one of them freak shots that ricocheted off a man's teeth, as had happened when Slade shot Jules Reni. This one shattered the bone and put Hardin in what must have been excruciating pain as he fell to the ground, dropping his pistol and letting out a wild yell of pain.

I turned sideways then, like you've seen them duelists do when they pace off and fire at each other, and shot Reitz just above the belt buckle. He staggered, and a look of shock came to his face at the same time a piece of lead tugged at my right thigh, surprising me as well. I don't know who did it, and I didn't care at the time, for Reitz was the one I was going to finish off. My second shot went right through his heart, and he died before he was halfway to the ground.

When Jim said he was ready to die, he meant it!

With a quick glance to my left I saw him standing there in full view of anyone who dared to potshot him, both guns out, both of them throwing lead like it was going out of style! The

Cajun jerked back twice before falling dead, a surprised look on his face. Rodell had caught one below the belt buckle and was in pain when he slowly raised his gun to shoot. Jim hit him in the gun arm, and the man dropped the pistol and fell to the ground, his hand over his intestines, a painful look about him.

My leg felt as if someone had stuck a white-hot bowie in and given it a good twist before pulling it out, but it was Jim who seemed to have blood all over him now. There was blood on his left arm and some on his leg too, but he walked forward in a calm, purposeful manner. Like I said, Jim was a *doer*, and he wasn't quitting on this job. Not a chance!

I followed him to where Rodell lay, writhing in agony as the heat from Jim's slug ate up his insides.

"You were ready to die . . . for this?" the man asked incredulously. "We could have had you. We could have—"

"Sorry bastards like you make one mistake, Rodell," Jim said, his guns hanging at his sides. He looked near death his own self, to tell the truth. "Time was when I'd have given a second thought about whether I might die. But, mister, you killed my *wife*, and after that I got nothing else to lose in this world, so you see, I don't give a damn."

Then he raised the Dragoon slowly, cocking it as he did, and shot the man through the heart.

"Like I said, mister, you're gonna wind up guarding the back gates of hell, and you don't need no heart to do that."

Three shots rang out in succession then. The first came from my rear, from Hardin, who had recovered his gun. It hit Jim in the right shoulder and was what seemed like the final shot to do him in as he fell to the ground. I was turning around, cocking that Navy as I did, when the second shot rang out. It came from the trees, and I saw Hardin's body jerk back to the earth before my own bullet tore out his brain. I reckon it was instinct that made me do it or maybe just the damndest will to survive after all that had happened that day, but I was cocking that Navy again, not even sure I had another bullet to fire as I aimed it at the trees where the shot had come from.

I needn't have bothered, for there, at the edge of the trees, was Rosa, slowly lowering a Hawken from her shoulder. Once again she had saved my life. She said nothing as she walked over to the bodies of the four dead men, silently examining them although she never once touched them. But it was Jim I was worried about now, and I reckon any Christian upbringing I had had sort of left me that day as I looked at her.

"Leave 'em," I said, a new hardness in my voice, a tone I'd never noticed before. "That's four pieces of meat ain't going to need no poison to kill them wolves."

Jim was still alive, although just barely. I couldn't tell for all the blood on him, but I'd wager he had at least four bullets in him. She helped me get him on a horse and somehow secured him to it. I don't know how I could have been of any use to her, as weak as I was feeling, but Jim was in far worse shape than me.

"You ride like hell, understand?" I said to her. It seemed to be a day for me giving orders. "Get him back there and doctor him best you can. I'll be along."

For a minute there I thought she was going to question me, not do as I bade. What she was doing, though, was studying me, in the damndest sort of way, kind of like Jim had done when we first left to get the remuda. Then a touch of a smile broke at the corners of her mouth, and she came to me and kissed me full on the mouth. When she stepped back, I wasn't sure if I was feeling weaker or stronger or what. Surprised was more like it. But the smile had grown wider on her face, and I knew she was happy about something when she stepped back.

"You are a good man" was all she said, and I reckon just then it felt worth hearing, it really did.

She had the reins of Jim's mount in her hand as she left at a good pace, going as fast as she dared without losing him. I watched her go and slowly climbed into my own saddle, aching all over now. I needed rest and plenty of it, but it was always the family first, and I had to get back to make sure Jim made it through all right. Us Callahans don't die too awful easy, you see.

It could have been days before I finally reached the clearing that led to the house, to what used to be called the Stiles station. Likely it was only an hour or so, and painful all the way. Still, I had to know about Jim. I walked the horse into the yard, seeing Alicia's body still on the porch, Aaron Stiles's still in front of the barn. I didn't think I was that noisy, but Rosa was on the steps in a second.

"He's a tough man." Weak as I was, it made me feel better to hear her say it.

"Yeah, there's that. But you got to remember, he's a—"

I never did finish speaking my piece. It was about then the ground met my face right close like and I passed out.

17

IT took two weeks of bed rest to get back on my feet. Both Jim and I had lost a lot of blood. Rosa said it was four slugs she had taken out of him. How he made it I'll never know, but I reckon she was right when she said he was one tough man.

Rogers, the wrangler who'd been hit in the original shoot-out, had been put in charge of the station and was breaking in a couple of new wranglers. And doing a pretty good job of it too.

By that time someone from the South had gotten tired of just talking and had fired on some place they called Fort Sumter in the Carolinas, and the whole nation was going to war—civil war. Word had it that the message delivered about the declaration of war by President Lincoln was the fastest one the Pony ever delivered, doing so in a record seven days. But that war was a thousand miles from where we were located, and it might as well have been a million, for it was still business as usual on the Pony.

I'd pretty much resigned myself to the fact that I'd soon have to be moving on, have to find something new because the telegraph lines were becoming more numerous with each passing day. And that meant the Pony Express and its days carrying the mail were numbered.

Jim didn't do much talking at all. It was like he had withdrawn from the world and didn't care to associate with it anymore. I knew he had Alicia on his mind, but I knew something else as well. What I had predicted, what I had thought might happen if he survived that last fight . . . well, it had happened. It wasn't right, and it shouldn't have been, but there's some things you can't change in people, especially when they've set their minds to it. And I had a feeling Jim Callahan had done just that. When he said he had lost any feeling for dying with the death of his wife, he was right. It was like he'd thrown the key in the bucket and chucked it down the well as far as his emotions went. And somehow I knew that he'd never be the same, never be the free, easygoing man I'd started this adventure with so long ago.

"Figured out what you're going to do?" I asked one day as we sat on the porch.

"I'm leaving this place, that's for sure," he said. I thought he swallowed hard saying it. "Don't know if I'll ever be able to stand the memories again. I'd rather have her."

"You are wrong." It was Rosa, standing in the doorway, who spoke now, apparently having overheard us. When Jim looked up at her with a critical eye, she continued. "You will *always* have her." She placed a hand over her breast, indicating her heart. "In here." Then, stepping out on the porch, she faced Jim.

"But it don't seem like I'll ever get away from her, no matter how far I travel from this place," he said, a desperate sound to his voice now.

"Your feeling is much like life. We go through it and make the mistake of thinking we must always remember everything. What is important, Jim, is that you remember the good times . . . and that you *never* forget them. That is best."

As quickly as she was there, she was gone. Jim didn't say much else then, mostly sat there thinking, I reckon. Me, I wasn't sure what it was Rosa was telling him, but she seemed like an almighty powerful woman when you got to talking about upstairs.

I don't know if it was what she said or if he sorted it out for himself, but Jim seemed in a better mood a few days later when we rolled our blankets and saddled fresh horses. I reckon I was in a bit better mood myself, but that was because of Rosa too. We all knew it was time to part ways, though, for the world had changed for each of us since a year ago. Everything had changed.

"Got any idea where you're heading?" Jim said, mounting up.

I shrugged. "Don't know about that war stuff. I figure I know Indians better than anything. And I've ridden enough of this land to know a good share of it. Reckon I'll go see Ma and see what old Kit Carson has to recommend. He's been out here a long time. How about you?"

"Don't want nothing to do with that war. Confusing as hell, to hear people talk about it. I done some thinking, though. Way I see it, a lot of people are going to get caught up in this war, a goodly number of them from out here, too."

"Then what are you going to do?"

"Well, I ain't much better than fair with these Dragoons, but I reckon someone's going to have to keep the likes of Rodell and the rest out of decent towns. Besides, I never was too impressed with the lawmen I seen west of the Mississippi. 'Bout time they had some backbone put into them, you ask me."

And he'd do that, Jim Callahan would. For he wasn't just fair with those pistols of his; he was damn good!

"I think you're doing the right thing," I said.

He nodded, and Rosa came out on the porch, and I could feel the back of my neck getting hot again.

"Say, Sean, are you blushing?" he asked.

I was looking at Rosa, knowing that it was goodbye and that I might never see her again, knowing that it could never be.

"Rosa," Jim said, "what's he blushing about?"

But she only smiled at me and said, "Some things are better left for nature to explain."

"Ma'am?"

"He knows," she said, still smiling warmly.

We rode out then, and of a sudden Jim's face

broke into a grin, and by God, I think he knew too.

Fact is, I know he did!

THE END

Books by Jim Miller
in the Linford Western Library:

COMANCHE TRAIL
WAR CLOUDS
RIDING SHOTGUN
SUNSETS
GONE TO TEXAS
CAMPAIGNING
ORPHANS PREFERRED

*Other titles in the
Linford Western Library:*

HELL RIDERS
by Steve Mensing

Wade Walker's kid brother, Duane, was locked up in the Silver City jail facing a rope at dawn. Wade was a ruthless outlaw, but he was smart, and he had vowed to have his brother out of jail before morning!

DESERT OF THE DAMNED
by Nelson Nye

The law was after him for the murder of a marshal—a murder he didn't commit. Breen was after him for revenge—and Breen wouldn't stop at anything . . . blackmail, a frameup . . . or murder.

DAY OF THE COMANCHEROS
by Steven C. Lawrence

Their very name struck terror into men's hearts—the Comancheros, a savage army of cutthroats who swept across Texas, leaving behind a bloodstained trail of robbery and murder.

SUNDANCE: SILENT ENEMY
by John Benteen

Both the Indians and the U.S. Cavalry were being victimized. A lone crazed Cheyenne was on a personal war path against both sides. They needed to pit one man against one crazed Indian. That man was Sundance.

LASSITER
by Jack Slade

Lassiter wasn't the kind of man to listen to reason. Cross him once and he'd hold a grudge for years to come—if he let you live that long. But he was no crueler than the men he had killed, and he had never killed a man who didn't need killing.

LAST STAGE TO GOMORRAH
by Barry Cord

Jeff Carter, tough ex-riverboat gambler, now had himself a horse ranch that kept him free from gunfights and card games. Until Sturvesant of Wells Fargo showed up. Jeff owed him a favour and Sturvesant wanted it paid up. All he had to do was to go to Gomorrah and recover a quarter of a million dollars stolen from a stagecoach!

McALLISTER ON THE COMANCHE CROSSING
by Matt Chisholm

The Comanche, deadly warriors and the finest horsemen in the world, reckon McAllister owes them a life—and the trail is soaked with the blood of the men who had tried to outrun them before.

QUICK-TRIGGER COUNTRY
by Clem Colt

Turkey Red hooked up with Curly Bill Graham's outlaw crew and soon made a name for himself. But wholesale murder was out of Turk's line, so when range war flared he bucked the whole border gang alone . . .

PISTOL LAW
by Paul Evan Lehman

Lance Jones came back to Mustang for just one thing—Revenge! Revenge on the people who had him thrown in jail; on the crooked marshal; on the human vulture who had already taken over the town. Now it was Lance's turn . . .

FARGO: MASSACRE RIVER
by John Benteen

Fargo spurred his horse to the edge of the road. The ambushers up ahead had now blocked the road. Fargo's convoy was a jumble, a perfect target for the insurgents' weapons!

SUNDANCE: DEATH IN THE LAVA
by John Benteen

The land echoed with the thundering hoofs of Modoc ponies. In minutes they swooped down and captured the wagon train and its cargo of gold. But now the halfbreed they called Sundance was going after it, and he swore nothing would stand in his way.

GUNS OF FURY
by Ernest Haycox

Dane Starr, alias Dan Smith, wanted to close the door on his past and hang up his guns, but people wouldn't let him. Good men wanted him to settle their scores for them. Bad men thought they were faster and itched to prove it. Starr had to keep killing just to stay alive.

FARGO: PANAMA GOLD
by John Benteen

Cleve Buckner was recruiting an army of killers, gunmen and deserters from all over Central America. With foreign money behind him, Buckner was going to destroy the Panama Canal before it could be completed. Fargo's job was to stop Buckner—and to eliminate him once and for all!

FARGO: THE SHARPSHOOTERS
by John Benteen

The Canfield clan, thirty strong, were raising hell in Texas. One of them had shot a Texas Ranger, and the Rangers had to bring in the killer. Fargo was tough enough to hold his own against the whole clan.

SUNDANCE: OVERKILL
by John Benteen

Sundance's reputation as a fighting man had spread. There was no job too tough for the halfbreed to handle. So when a wealthy banker's daughter was kidnapped by the Cheyenne, he offered Sundance $10,000 to rescue the girl.

MBkm 6/95-11/95
M2 11/95-9/96